MURDER, MAJORCAN STYLE

MURDER, MAJORCAN STYLE

Roderic Jeffries

M JEFFRIES
J AUG 2011

This first world edition published 2011
in Great Britain and in the USA by
SEVERN HOUSE PUBLISHERS LTD of
9–15 High Street, Sutton, Surrey, England, SM1 1DF.
Trade paperback edition first published
in Great Britain and the USA 2011 by
SEVERN HOUSE PUBLISHERS LTD .

British Library Cataloguing in Publication Data

Jeffries, Roderic, 1926-
    Murder, Majorcan style. – (An Inspector Alvarez mystery)
    1. Alvarez, Enrique (Fictitious character)–Fiction.
    2. Police–Spain–Majorca–Fiction. 3. Detective and
    mystery stories.
    I. Title II. Series
    823.9'14-dc22

ISBN-13: 978-0-7278-8043-7   (cased)
ISBN-13: 978-1-84751-355-7   (trade paper)

All Severn House titles are printed on acid-free paper.

Severn House Publishers support The Forest Stewardship Council [FSC],
the leading international forest certification organisation. All our titles that
are printed on Greenpeace-approved FSC-certified paper carry the FSC logo.

FSC® MIX
Paper from
responsible sources
FSC www.fsc.org   FSC® C018575

Typeset by Palimpsest Book Production Ltd.,
Falkirk, Stirlingshire, Scotland.
Printed and bound in Great Britain by
MPG Books Ltd., Bodmin, Cornwall.

ONE

Sunshine came through the single window and illuminated the layered fog from the green Jaguar's exhaust and part of the figure of the man who had slumped forward and who sprawled across the steering wheel.

In his office, Alvarez considered what Dolores might be cooking for supper. It was a long while since they had enjoyed Fava parada, one of his many favourite meals. Once, a typical dish of peasant farmers, in her hands it would grace a five-star restaurant. He looked at his watch and was dismayed that the time was only just after five. Three hours before he would be expected to leave the office, at least an hour and a half before he did so and could reasonably explain his absence if called upon to do so.

The phone rang. He hesitated, instinctively certain this meant trouble. Since it continued, he finally lifted the receiver. 'Llueso Cuerpo . . .' he began.

'Caught you just before you skulked off early?'

'Who's that?'

'The Prime Minister's third secretary wishing to congratulate you on completing twenty years' service without achieving anything.'

He recognized the voice. Tomeu, a policia in Port Llueso with whom he had often enjoyed an evening of fun. 'It is an offence to show disrespect towards a member of the Cuerpo.'

'How does one have respect for a man who switches his affections with monotonous regularity?'

'I tell her how much I earn and she does the switching.'

'But not until she starts talking about the joys of motherhood? How are Dolores and Jaime?'

When family news had been exhausted, Tomeu said: 'D'you know Ca'n Mortex on the bay road?'

'The large stone house a retired general had built years ago, which has been bought by a foreigner who's planted mature palm trees at some phenomenal cost?'

'Englishman. Like all his tribe, offer them sunshine and they lose any thoughts about the value of money.'

'What about the place?'

'This is about the owner. Señor Sterne has been found dead in his car in the garage. The engine was switched on, the tank was empty of fuel. He's slumped over the wheel and not driving anywhere any more.'

'The usual rubber hose from exhaust to the interior of the car?'

'No. It's a large car and a small garage for the size of the house. It would have filled with exhaust fumes pretty quickly. From what I remember about a case some years back, it's the carbon monoxide which does the damage and that doesn't have to be strong before it quickly makes one too drowsy and muddled to do anything.'

'Who's living in the house?'

'A brother and sister, adult children of the dead man. She's pure bitch. Then there's a couple and their daughter who do the housework.'

'What have you learned from them?'

'I've left it to you to do the questioning. That's supposed to be your job.'

'Is Doctor Antignac there yet?'

'I reckoned it best if you called him.'

'What about a photographer?'

'Your pigeon.'

'Every task is someone else's?'

Tomeu laughed.

Alvarez replaced the receiver with more force than was necessary. Gone was a quiet evening, the pleasure of a drink, or two, before a delicious meal (Fava parada?). He was faced with work, would probably return home long after the meal was served so that his portion would have to be reheated and would consist only of what the family had left. And in the immediate future, he must phone Superior Chief Salas.

He dialled Palma. When contact was made, he asked: 'Is the superior chief still in his office?'

'Naturally!' Ángela Torres, Salas' secretary, expressed her contempt for anyone who could imagine he would leave the office early.

'I need to speak to him.'

'Who is calling?'

She would know perfectly well who he was, but she needed to remind any caller that she was the virginal go-between on whose shoulders rested the efficient running of the corps.

'Inspector Alvarez, señorita.'

'It helps to know who the caller is.'

There was a pause, then Salas said, in his usual abrupt manner: 'Yes?'

'Inspector Alvarez, señor.'

'There is no need to waste time by unnecessarily identifying yourself.'

'I was just making certain you knew it was me.'

'It was I.'

There was a longer pause. Finally, Salas said: 'Like Exmorodes, you have been stricken dumb?'

'I can't quite understand what you meant when you said you were you?'

'I was trying to correct you to say, it was I.'

'But I know who I am.'

'I have no intention of trying to unravel your incomprehensible nonsense. I will ask you questions, you will answer them briefly and without any prevarication. Why are you phoning?'

'To make a report.'

'What is hindering you?'

'When you said . . .?'

'Your report.'

'An Englishman, Señor Sterne, who lived at Ca'n Mortex, in Port Llueso, has committed suicide, gassing himself in his car.'

'In the usual manner?'

'Apparently not.'

'Why do you say "apparently"?'

'I haven't yet visited the property to confirm the facts.'

'You can see no reason to have done so?'

'In the circumstances, it seemed more important to inform you first.'

'The forensic doctor confirms your judgement?'

'He hasn't yet examined the dead man.'

'You have no direct confirmation the man is dead because you have not bothered to observe his body or the circumstances which surround it, yet you confidently state this is a case of suicide?'

'The petrol tank is empty and the ignition is switched on.'

'Facts you have accessed intuitively?'

'One of the policia in the port has reported them to me.'

'It is reassuring to learn there is someone who understands how a case should be conducted. Do you consider it might be an idea not to waste much more time before learning what the doctor has to say and to find out for yourself what are the facts?'

'I intend to drive down to the port the moment I finish speaking to you, señor.'

'You will not find that too precipitous an action?' Salas closed the line.

Alvarez replaced the receiver, sighed. Being a Madrileño, Salas would never appreciate that to rush was to shorten one's life.

TWO

C a'n Mortex was large and slab-like; being rock-built, many of the windows were small; except for the roof, there were only right angles; it would have been easy to be mistaken into believing it had been intended to offer defence from sea marauders as well as being a home.

Alvarez drove past the wrought-iron gates of elaborate design, the costly replanted palm trees, the multicoloured flower beds, braked to a halt in front of the portico with elaborate columns and pediment. He stepped out of the car, paused to look back across the garden and road at the bay.

The water was poster blue, the sunshine softened the appearance of the surrounding mountains, the slight breeze only fitfully filled the sails of yachts and windsurfers.

There was a polished brass knocker on the panelled door. As he struck it, the deep, dissonant sound reminded him, for no apparent reason, of Riera's poem, 'Time past as time present', which he had had to learn word perfect at school. He had never understood it.

The door opened with a couple of creaks and a youngish man, dressed in white jacket and striped linen trousers, said, 'Yes?' in a tone of sharp disparagement.

Alvarez had forgotten to shave that morning, he might with advantage have changed his shirt, but that provided no reason to assume he was an undesirable visitor. Many Mallorquins, especially those employed by foreigners, had forgotten the old saying, gold marks the wealthy man, manners the gentleman. 'Inspector Alvarez, Cuerpo General de Policia,' he answered sharply.

The change in manner was immediate. 'I'm sorry, Inspector, unfortunately I did not recognize you.'

'Perhaps because you have never met me.' A response worthy of Salas?

'Please come in.'

Rank could be as effective as gold in marking superiority.

He entered a large, vaulted hall. A waste of space in his philistine judgement. The floor was tiled in island marble; in the centre was a richly coloured and patterned carpet; there were several doors, each made from rich wood in traditional patterns; there was a large cut-glass bowl filled with flowers, adding the lightness of colour to an otherwise bleak appearance.

'Will you come into the green sitting-room, Inspector?'

He entered. A large room, predominately coloured green, so carefully furnished with antique and quality furniture, it seemed to him to be more like an advertisement in a glossy magazine than a place to relax.

'Can I have your name?' Alvarez asked, as he stood by a luxuriously upholstered settee.

'Evaristo Roldan.'

'What other staff are there?'

'My wife and my daughter work in the house, Marcial in the garden.'

'Is he full-time?'

'Necessarily so. As well as the flower beds in the front of the house, there is a large vegetable garden at the back.'

'Unusual for a foreigner to bother to grow vegetables.'

'There were lawns, but Señor Sterne wanted fresh vegetables grown from English seeds. He liked to have them as fresh as possible; said that was the only way to enjoy them as they should taste.'

'A gourmet of vegetables.'

'Of all food.'

'What relatives or friends of the dead man are staying or living here?'

'Señor Alec Sterne and Señorita Caroline Sterne, his son and daughter, have been here for some little time. There are no guests.'

'Where are they?'

'They left earlier.'

'Do you know when they intend to return?'

'I'm afraid not.'

'The señor was married?'

'His wife does not live on the island.'

'Divorced?'

'I believe so.'

'Does he have a girlfriend here?'

'Yes. Which is to say . . .'

'Then say it.'

'I don't think it is my position to do so.'

'Have another think.'

'He has entertained more than one lady.'

'Who found the señor?'

'I did.'

'In what circumstances?'

'He'd said he'd be out for lunch and so when, soon after his son and daughter had left, there was a phone call, I answered it. A lady wanted to know where he was because he had failed to meet her.'

'Who was she?'

'She didn't give her name, but from her voice I thought she might be Cecilia.'

'Her surname?'

'I have never heard it.'

'One of his girlfriends?'

'It seemed likely.'

'Especially when they came down together to breakfast? Do you know if she's married?'

'I believe so.'

'When she said he hadn't turned up, did you wonder if something might have happened to him?'

'I just thought he had changed his mind.'

'About lunch or Cecilia?'

'It could have been either.'

'Then what?'

'Later on, I needed a screwdriver – tools are kept in the garage. Even before I opened the interior door, I could smell exhaust fumes. When I switched on the light, I could see the señor slumped over the wheel.'

'So you did what?'

'Put a handkerchief over my nose, went down into the garage, smashed the window with an axe, opened the outside doors.

I saw the señor was dead so I returned into the house and phoned the policia.'

'How did you know he was dead?'

'His face . . . He'd vomited. He was so . . . so lifeless.'

'You didn't open the car door and feel his pulse or heart.'

'No, because . . . I was so certain.'

Alvarez could well understand the reluctance to touch the body of a man one thought was dead; he had to nerve himself to do that when it became necessary. 'I need to go into the garage.'

'Then will you follow me, Inspector.'

They went out into the hall and across to the far right-hand door.

'D'you want me to come down with you?' Roldan asked.

'Best if you stay here.'

There were five steps down to the floor of the garage which was small, considering the size of the house – when that had been built, cars had been rare on the island, two-car owners unknown.

The air, though apparently clear, still contained the smell of exhaust fumes despite the smashed window and opened garage doors. He studied the red Jaguar and, with reluctance, the body inside. Another's death was a harbinger of one's own limited lifespan. The previous night, after supper, he had suffered pain in the stomach. The consequence of an overgenerous supper, or a forewarning?

It was not surprising Roldan had accepted Sterne was dead. To look at his face, his body sprawled forward across the wheel, forehead against the windscreen, the condition of the car inside, left no doubt. He opened the front passenger door, lowered the window, releasing a brief, strong smell of exhaust fumes. He examined the dashboard. All the dials had zeroed. He used a handkerchief to check the ignition key was fully turned on.

There was no suicide note on the seats, in the glove locker or the side pockets of the doors.

Not all suicides left behind expressions of dislike of someone or something.

The photographer arrived and at Alvarez's orders, took

photographs of the dead man from several angles. A minute after he had left, there was a call from outside the garage. 'Señor, Doctor Antignac has arrived.'

He walked along the side of the car to meet Antignac by the open doors. They shook hands, briefly commented on how long it had been since they last met. Unlike many doctors, Antignac was friendly and did not display a suggestion of inherent omniscience.

'What have we got?' he asked. 'My secretary said that whoever phoned, spoke very confusingly.'

'It's a suicide. Gassed himself in the car.'

'Who's the victim?'

'The owner of the property, Señor Sterne.'

'I think I met him some time back – socially, not professionally. Spoke quite reasonable Spanish for an Englishman.'

Antignac walked forward until level with the front car door, which he opened. He studied the body, examined the head, reached inside to lift the lightweight T-shirt, shifted the body to carry out a temperature investigation. He stepped back. 'He did not die from carbon monoxide poisoning.'

Alvarez spoke impulsively. 'He must have done.'

'A professional difference of opinion?' A brief smile.

'But . . . There's still the stink of exhaust fumes.'

'Had he died from monoxide poisoning, his skin would be discoloured cherry red. There is no hint of this.'

'Then was it a heart attack?' He spoke hopefully. A natural death would entail far less work than would suicide.

'The post-mortem will have to decide on that. However, there is an injury to his head.'

'He may have been attacked?'

'One can never be certain from a surface examination, but I think it will be found to be relatively minor and most unlikely to have caused death, so an attack seems doubtful. The time of death, inaccurate as ever when judged by the spread of rigor and the temperature of the body, was between ten and twelve hours ago. You will have remarked the somewhat sideways manner in which he rests in the car?'

He had noticed this, but had been too preoccupied to accord it any significance.

'It is not a position in which one normally sits behind a wheel, but perhaps suggests a slump after seating. The dust and dirt on the back of his shirt and trousers may well mean he was lying on something pretty dirty before his death.'

'What do you reckon that signifies?'

'I have always found it expedient to leave a qualified person to answer the question when his skill is required.' He smiled, robbing his words of implied criticism. 'You can arrange for the body to be taken to the morgue.' He shook hands, left the garage.

With disrespectful annoyance, Alvarez stared at the body as the doctor drove away. A simple suicide had seemingly become a complicated question mark. Sterne had not died of monoxide poisoning, had an injury to his head, had been lying somewhere dirty before his death . . .

He became more cheerful. A heart attack would explain everything. As Sterne entered the garage, an initial shaft of pain caused him to lurch forward and bang his head on something which projected. To overcome his confused fears, he had lain down on the garage floor. Recovering, he had climbed into the car, started the engine, realized the garage doors were still closed, reached across for the remote control to open them, suffered a second and fatal attack.

He returned to the hall, called out. Roldan hurried into view. 'Sorry, Inspector, but I was helping Marta, my wife.'

'Have you had any further word from the brother or sister to suggest when they'll be back?'

'No.'

'It will be better if they don't return before the body is moved. It might well affect them very badly.'

'It will deeply upset Señor Sterne . . . That is, Señor Alec.'

'Not the sister?'

'She has a stronger character. Is there anything more I can do for you?'

'Not for now, thanks.'

Alvarez was amused to note how Roldan's manner contrasted sharply with what it had been on his arrival. Show a mule who was boss and there'd be no trouble.

*   *   *

For once, there was parking space immediately in front of No. 16. Alvarez used his key to unlock the front door – property could no longer be left unsecured without fear of theft, due to the depredations of foreigners, illegal immigrants, and drugs.

The entrada was dust free and immaculately tidy, the furniture was newly polished, fresh flowers were on the ancient dough-mixer. A housewife's ability was judged by the condition of her entrada.

Jaime was in the sitting/dining-room; he sat at the table, in front of a glass and a bottle of Fundador. Alvarez settled on the opposite side of the table. 'It's very quiet. Where are the kids?'

'How would I know?'

Dolores called out from the kitchen. 'Why ask him when his only interest is in drinking? Isabel and Juan are having lunch with a friend.'

Alvarez reached down to open the Mallorquin sideboard, brought out a glass, filled it with brandy and four cubes of ice.

Dolores stepped through the bead curtain across the doorway. One of the strings of beads became caught on her shoulder; she cast if off with a forceful gesture. She wore a recently stained apron over a working dress, her midnight hair was in slight disarray, her only jewellery was her wedding ring, her only ornament, the crude novelty brooch which Isabel and Juan had given her after their visit to the Christmas fair. Because they had bought this at the expense of sweets for themselves, she wore the brooch with the same pride as a rider at the Feria, dressed immaculately on a horse of impeccable pedigree, displayed herself. 'I've something I wish to tell you, Enrique.'

Alvarez failed to judge from the tone of her voice whether the something was likely to be unwelcome.

'I met Ana Loup when I was shopping.'

His concern had been unnecessary. 'How is her arm?'

'Why do you ask that?'

'Someone told me she had broken it.'

'You are thinking of Ana Barrio who tripped over a box because of her husband's thoughtless stupidity.'

'According to Felix,' Jaime remarked, 'it was entirely her own fault. He'd warned her it was there.'

'As my dear mother used to say, "A man will blame an angel rather than himself."' She turned to Alvarez. 'She asked how you were and was glad to hear you were well.'

'That was friendly of her.'

'Typical!' She stared sharply at him, returned into the kitchen.

Alvarez leaned across the edge of the table in order to be able to speak in a low voice. Dolores had the female ability to hear what was not intended for her ears. 'Who's Ana Loup?'

Jaime did not lower his voice sufficiently. 'No idea.'

Dolores reappeared. 'You have no idea about what?' She was not answered. She addressed Alvarez. 'Were you asking who Ana is?' There was now frost in her voice. 'You do not remember her?'

He tried to divert her annoyance. 'The name does seem to ring a bell.'

'Very faintly.'

'One meets so many people in my job, it takes a little time to sort out who someone is.'

'You have no great reason to remember her? Perhaps you cannot differentiate her from the many women who have the misfortune to be in your memory.' She turned, went back into the kitchen.

Alvarez drained his glass, refilled it, offered Jaime a cigarette before lighting his own. Ana Barrio was the only Ana he could recall.

'Have you laid the table?' Dolores called out.

After a quick look at the bead curtain, Jaime refilled his glass. 'Lay the table . . . Won't give a man a moment's peace. Expect us to do everything while they fiddle around.'

She reappeared, studied the table. 'You do not intend to eat?'

'How d'you mean?' Jaime asked.

'Lacking plate, knife and fork, you will find eating difficult and the slightest difficulty defeats you.'

They ate Greixonera d'anguiles, a dish from Mestara which was the only place on the island where eels were found. She cleared the table, returned with clean plates, oranges and baked almonds. She sat, helped herself to several almonds, did not immediately eat. 'You have decided to remember Ana?'

'I still can't place her,' Alvarez answered reluctantly.

'You clearly choose not to do so.'

He peeled an orange.

'As Ricardo Fons wrote, "When a man admits to ignorance, it is because he fears the truth." And after what Ana mentioned, you clearly have every reason to fear the truth.'

'So what did she tell you?'

She ate.

'If you won't explain, how can I understand what you're going on about?'

'Conscience makes many cowards.' She ate two almonds. 'In an age when so many are concerned only with themselves, it is uplifting to meet someone of such a forgiving nature. Had it been me, I would not have concerned myself with your well-being. That would be a matter of total indifference.'

Having washed-up, tidied the kitchen and the sitting room, Dolores left the house to collect Isabel and Juan. As he heard the front door close, Jaime poured himself another brandy and dropped three ice cubes into the glass. 'You're in the doghouse.' He passed the bottle across the table.

'I'm damned if I know why,' Alvarez said.

'You don't fool me, any more than you did her.'

'Can't you understand, I don't remember an Ana Loup.'

'And don't want to. It's obvious that when you were a lot younger, you had fun with her. And being female, she had to tell another woman all the details.'

If he did have fun, Alvarez thought, he might at least have been allowed the pleasure of the memory.

THREE

Alvarez awoke and initially enjoyed the pleasure of doing nothing, then remembered he would have to speak to Salas on his return to the office. He stared up at the ceiling, partially criss-crossed with reflected sunshine coming up through the shutters, and wondered why life was so unfair.

He had a shower and went downstairs, expecting to enjoy a breakfast of hot chocolate and perhaps a newly baked ensaimada from the nearby baker. There was a note on the dining-room table, written with some difficulty because Dolores had missed the schooling which a later generation were able to enjoy. She had had to leave home early to help a friend who was ill. Since he was so late getting up, he must get his own breakfast.

Uncertain how to make the rich chocolate he enjoyed, he decided to have coffee. After a brief examination of the electric percolator, he was able to judge how it worked. Since there was no ensaimada, he tried to make himself some Pa amb oli. He toasted the pan moreno, drizzled this with olive oil, rubbed it with a halved bush tomato. The result did not taste as it would have done had Dolores made it. The coffee was weak. A poor breakfast. He understood it was reasonable for her to help a friend, nevertheless . . .

He drove to the office, sat at his desk. It was necessary to steady his confidence. He opened the bottom right-hand drawer of the desk, brought out a nearly empty bottle of 103 and a glass. The bottle was empty before he phoned Palma.

'Doctor Antignac has examined the dead man, señor. It seems there is a problem.'

'How unusual!' Salas spoke sarcastically.

'Señor Sterne did not die from monoxide poisoning.'

'It is as well I do not expect you to corroborate facts before presenting them.'

'But he was found dead in the car and the garage was filled with exhaust fumes.'

'A man found dead in a bath obviously drowned?'

'It did seem . . .'

'Since you thought it unnecessary to visit the scene, the impossible would have seemed likely to you. Would it trouble you to inform me what was Doctor Antignac's judgement as to the cause of death, without putting your own interpretation on his words?'

'There was a small injury to the deceased's head. But the doctor was reasonably certain that was not the cause of death. As I had noted, the dead man sat partially sideways, not what one would normally expect, because of discomfort. However, this would be explained by his having suffered a heart attack as he closed, or immediately after he closed, the driving door. We won't know until after the post-mortem.'

'The doctor cannot give the possible cause of death?'

'No, señor.'

'Then what did he say it was?'

'I have just explained, that won't be known until the post-mortem.'

'You've just said he has given a cause.'

'I was agreeing that he cannot give a cause.'

'Then why didn't you answer "yes" to my question?'

'Surely that would have sounded as if he had given one?'

'You destroy the belief that speech enables meaningful communication. Is there anything else to report?'

'No, señor.'

'That is not intended to infer you have something?'

'Yes, it isn't.'

Salas replaced the receiver.

Alvarez went to pour himself a reviving brandy, was reminded the bottle was empty. He decided to have an early merienda.

He left the post, crossed the old square, filled with idle tourists seated at shaded tables and indulging themselves, went into Club Llueso.

Roca, behind the bar, said: 'Looking at you makes it certain you haven't won the lottery.'

'You think I'd be here if I had?'

'You'd want a bar with crystal glasses, Krug champagne, and whatever else the nouveau riche think they ought to like?'

'I'd find a bar with a competent, dumb barman. As it is, I'll have coffee cortado and a decent sized coñac.'

'You've brought a tankard to pour it into?'

When served, Alvarez turned to look through the window at the passing tourists, noted a couple arm-in-arm. She was celebrity attractive – thin, long-legged and in danger of losing modesty if she leaned too far forward. Years ago, she would have been arrested for wearing indecent clothing.

'You'd be wasting your time,' Roca said, as he put a glass, cup, and saucer down on the bar.

'Not if I'd won the lottery.'

'She'd have you as a sugar-daddy?'

Alvarez stopped in front of the portico entrance of Ca'n Mortex, climbed out of the car, stood by the opened door and stared at the bay. Natural beauty could never be dimmed by familiarity; it possessed the potential to redeem failure, soothe the troubled soul, restore pleasure to life; it possibly could even introduce Salas to humanity.

He finally turned back, crossed to the entrance and was about to knock when Roldan opened the door. 'Good morning, Inspector.'

Gone was the hint of snobbish superiority assumed by those who served the rich or famous. 'Morning.'

'Can I help you?'

'I'd like a word.'

'Please enter.'

As he stepped into the hall, a young woman, with a duster in her hand, and an older woman wheeling a Dyson, came out of a room.

'My wife, Marta, and daughter, Susanna,' Roldan said in introduction. 'Inspector Alvarez.' They nodded, continued across the hall and went into another room.

The twists of nature were serpentine, Alvarez thought. Marta, whilst probably not yet quite middle-aged, had unremarkable features and a figure which suggested a love of rich food. But her daughter might have been born rising from the sea. Susanna was garlanded with wavy, bronze-coloured hair, had an oval face of classical symmetry, eyes a lustrous blue, nose a Phidias masterpiece, lips of promise, a neck to shame a swan. Yet, possessed of such natural beauty, her expression had been bitter discontent.

'Would you come this way, Inspector, into the staff sitting-room.'

It was square and stark because of the stone walls which were bare, the furniture had the look of having descended from the owner's quarters.

They sat. Alvarez said: 'I want to know about Señor Sterne's lifestyle. Whether he had many friends, were there people he did not get on with. So tell me what you can.'

'I only know what I have learned in the normal course of my duties.'

'I'd not expect otherwise.' Yet had not Roldan 'spied' on his employer as did many employees who sought reason to scorn their employers? 'You are not from the island, are you?'

Roldan's accent and sing-song form of speech marked him a forestero.

'I was born and lived in Burgos.' Knowing the antipathy to a 'forestero' – anyone not from the island, even if Spanish – he added: 'Work became difficult and we were told it would be easier to find a job here.'

And more profitable when one found a foreigner who knowingly or unknowingly, paid an above-average wage. 'You have always been in service?' Any islander would regard the question to be insulting. A Mallorquin did not serve, he worked for someone.

Roldan showed no sign of resentment. 'There was a rich man in Burgos whose butler wanted an assistant and I gained the job. After a couple of years, I married and Marta was employed as the cook. The owner died suddenly, we then had a daughter, so needed to find another position as quickly as possible and came to the island.'

'Your wife is also from Galicia?'

'Yes.'

'Does she cook Angulas en cazuelita?' A dish with a taste beyond description. Baby eels from Aguinaga, and nowhere else, garlic, pimiento . . .

'The señor so liked the dish, he had the angulas sent down here. There was a batch due in two days, but we have cancelled it.'

A mistake. Had they forgotten to do so, the batch would have arrived and they might well have seen fit to share them with another.

'The señor is divorced and his ex-wife does not come here?'

'I have not known her do so.'

'Did you like the señor?'

'I think it sensible never to like or dislike the person for whom one works.'

Those who worked for Salas had no such reservation. 'Did he pay well?'

'Isn't that a matter of opinion, Inspector?'

'Your opinion is?'

'He thought he bought more than he paid for.'

Alvarez was surprised by the bitterness of Roldan's reply. Made to work a great deal of unpaid overtime? 'You've told me he did not have many friends.'

'He gave dinner and cocktail parties, but not often and I would not say there were ever a large number of guests.'

'In a place like this, one would expect endless parties. Why d'you think there weren't?'

'Difficult to say.'

'Was he not a well-liked man because he was rich? That always creates jealous dislike.'

Roldan spoke slowly. 'I understand the English have the reputation of being small-minded over some things.'

'Such as?'

'Behaviour.'

'Did he dress like a tramp, swear in front of women, spit in the street?'

'He was always meticulously well dressed and mannered.'

'You appear to be contradicting yourself. If he was so present-able, why did people – the English – have reason to criticize him?'

'I should prefer not to pursue the matter.'

'I fear your preference matters zilch.'

'The señor enjoyed the company of many ladies.'

'Why the hesitation in telling me that? What's the worth of money if you don't enjoy its products?'

'I think one should not speak ill of the dead.'

'Often there's not much else to say about them. Throttle your conscience and tell me about these women.'

'Until recently, he frequently brought a lady back who spent the night, or several nights, here.'

'"Until recently." What slowed him down?'

'I can only surmise.'

'Do so.'

'Señorita Janet was here many times and he seemed to become closely attached to her and her to him.'

'As one would expect.'

Roldan ignored the comment. 'Then something happened to upset the relationship.'

'What?'

'I think . . .' Roldan stopped.

'Getting information out of you is like trying to squeeze juice out of a last year's orange.'

'It's not easy to break one's sense of loyalty.'

'Think of me as being in the position of a priest, ready to absolve your conscience. He got fed up with her?'

'It was the other way round. She left here to go to England for a few days and when she returned there was a sharp disagreement.'

'Your way of saying they had a hell of a row? What was that over?'

'They spoke so loudly, I could not help overhearing them.'

'Tell me what you inadvertently heard.'

'She accused him of entertaining another woman whilst she was away.'

'Had he?'

'It wasn't really his fault.'

'Never is the man's.'

'A very attractive woman whom he'd known before arrived and said she wanted to see the señor. I didn't know what to do. I mean, we all liked Janet. But he came out of a room, saw her, and that was that.

'She left the next morning, shortly before Señorita Janet was due back. And when Señorita Janet was here, she discovered what had been happening.'

'How?'

'The señor had persuaded the other señorita to stay longer than she should have done and so she had to leave in a real hurry in a taxi. Unfortunately, in the rush she left evidence of having been there.'

'Señorita Janet left him for good?'

'Yes.'

'And he returned to variety?'

'He has not entertained a young lady since she left.'

That suggested he was genuinely fond of her, but could he have been when he had someone else in his bed while she was away? Of course, men saw things in a very much more sensible light than did women. 'After she left him, what sort of a mood was he in?'

'Unhappy.'

'Having learned a bird in hand is worth several in the bush. What was her surname?'

'We never learned it.'

'Was she married?'

'She wore no marriage ring.'

'Have you or the others found any kind of suicide note in the house?'

'If any of us had, Inspector, we would have said so immediately.'

'Is there anything more you can tell me about what went on that night which might be relevant?'

'Can't think of anything. That is unless . . . But the car can't have been of any importance.'

'What car?'

'It drove out soon after the brother and sister left.'

'You didn't hear it come in?'

'I'd been at the back of the house with the wife and daughter and you don't hear anything there.'

'No one had rung or knocked?'

'I never heard the bell ring, but recently it has occasionally malfunctioned. I reckoned the driver got no response and thought there was no one here.'

'How did you come to see him leave?'

'I'd gone into the breakfast room to check that it was all in order and saw it through the window.'

'Could you see the driver?'

'Only the back of his head.'

'Don't suppose you noticed the registration number?'

'Didn't think there was any reason to do that.'

'What make and colour was the car?'

'A black hatchback and likely a Citröen.'

'Was there anything unusual about it?'

'Only one of those dangling things inside the back window; daft in a saloon, dafter in a hatchback.'

'Is there a study here?'

'There is a library, which is where the señor often worked.'

'Have you been in there this morning?'

'No, but probably Susanna gave it a dust.'

'I'd like to see it.'

The stone staircase, with wooden banisters, was steep. The landing stretched in either direction and Roldan turned right, went into a square room which looked out at the mountains. There was a large, filled bookcase, a desk, clearly not of local manufacture, on which was a computer, keyboard, VDU and printer; two leather seated chairs; three filing cabinets, a large, free-standing safe, and on the walls, three framed prints of English hunting scenes and an oil painting of confused colour and no form.

'That's all the help I need for the moment,' Alvarez said.

Roldan left.

There was no suicide note amongst the loose papers on the desk or in any of the drawers. He searched under the desk to check whether the safe keys were concealed there, found nothing. If the staff had no idea where the keys were kept – as was to be expected – a locksmith would have to be called.

The morning was well advanced, so it was more sensible to return home, have lunch, a short siesta, and then resume work.

FOUR

The Pollo al ajillo was good, but with thoughts of Angulas en cazuelita . . .

'What is the matter?' Dolores asked.

'Nothing,' Alvarez answered.

'You have not asked if there is any more.'

'He's suddenly discovered table manners,' Jaime said.

Juan giggled. 'He eats with his mouth open.'

'It is not good manners to comment on bad manners,' she observed sharply.

'So there!' Isabel said.

'You eat like a camel,' Juan told his sister.

'If you two have anything more to say, you'll do so in your bedrooms,' Dolores threatened.

Jaime said: 'If they are in their own bedrooms, they won't be able to say anything to each other.'

'There are times when a wife has to wonder if her husband is trying to be unhelpful or incapable of understanding he is not.'

'You did say . . .'

She interrupted him. 'Enrique, I had coffee in the old square this morning.'

He could not decide why she told him this.

'With Ana.'

He understood.

'Which Ana?' Juan asked.

'Ana Loup, a friend of Uncle Enrique's.'

'Is she one of his pretty ladies?'

'A carefully forgotten companion,' Jaime suggested.

'There are many advantages to having a husband who works away from home,' Dolores remarked. She collected up the plates, told Isabel and Juan to bring them and the dishes into the kitchen, left the table.

'The children have gone off to have an ice cream,' she said, as she returned with several apples and three clean plates. 'Ana again asked how you were, Enrique.'

'She thought I might have fallen down a well?'

'You regard good manners with the same contempt as my husband?'

'If I don't remember her, I can't think why she keeps asking how I am.'

'She has a forgiving nature and hopes you are in good health. I do not expect you to understand.'

There was a brief silence, which she broke. 'She spoke frankly about her unhappy marriage.'

'Was that good manners?' Alvarez asked.

'Being a man, you talk very stupidly. She had been very unhappy, as one would expect, having been treated so cruelly when younger, as you have reason to know. Her friends were married and she was not getting younger, so when she met Emilio and he was very kind, she was pleased when he proposed.' She began to peel an apple. 'Would that women could learn in time that the man who proposes is not the man she marries.

'It is our misfortune to be blinded by deceitful emotion. Emilio began to drink heavily and all the work on the farm had to be done by the two farmhands. It was sad for her to see him slumped in a chair when he should be out in the fields . . . Aiyee! – has there ever been a man who considers someone else before himself?' She ate.

'This woman . . . Ana,' Alvarez hastily corrected himself, 'comes from farming stock?'

'Her parents soon died, so she had to learn how to run the estate. Emilio had said he would do that better than it had ever been run before. What he meant was, he would drink more than anyone had before. Only a woman could possess the courage and determination she possesses. Since Emilio died, she has been able to buy many more hectares of land on which to run more sheep and to grow their feed, she has planted many algarroba trees to meet the demand for their beans, she has made the farm as profitable as any on the island.'

'It must be a pretty big place,' Alvarez observed, interested, as always, in farming. 'Whereabouts is it?'

'She did not say.'

'Did she mention any nearby village?'

'If so, I have forgotten. You can ask her when you meet her.'

'Since that's very unlikely . . .'

'She is coming here for a meal.'

'Why?'

'I asked her.'

'When?'

'As soon as it is convenient to both of us. Considering your previous behaviour, I did not consider it necessary to consider you.'

There were times, Alvarez acknowledged, when a man was neither master of his own fate nor captain of his soul.

He sat behind the desk in the library at Ca'n Mortex, but his mind was far from his work. Having inherited an estate, Ana had not been from poor farming stock, which eliminated many females he could remember. Most of her friends had been married, so she was no chicken. He could not capture even a possible, if unlikely, memory of her.

The unknown was always to be avoided. When he was told the hour of her visit, he would arrange for a cabo to phone home at the appropriate time and express his apologies and say the superior chief had demanded he remain at work.

The problem considered and solved, he opened the folder in front of himself marked 'Local banks'. Chronologically arranged statements showed four thousand euros in the accounts and a monthly input of three thousand euros.

When that wealthy, a man could farm for pleasure, not profit. An unseasonable downpour might wash away all the sprouting corn, but this would not create the spectre of ruin; worn-out orange and lemon trees could be replaced; centuries-old olive trees with gnarled and twisted trunks could be tended with far more care than was warranted by the worth of their crop; varieties of seeds could be planted which favoured flavour, not maximum quantity – tomatoes, peppers, onions, potatoes, carrots, parsnips, beetroot, lettuces, melons, strawberries which tasted as they once had.

The phone rang, then stopped. It brought daydreams to an end, but did provide the brief pleasure of knowing the call could not concern him.

There was a knock on the door, Roldan stepped into the room. 'It is for you, Inspector.'

'Who is it?'

'I thought it best not to ask.'

He turned to leave.

'I'd like another word as soon as the call is over.'

'If you will use the buzzer on the desk, I will be along as quickly as possible.'

As Roldan left, Alvarez lifted the receiver.

'Taken so long to get hold of you, I reckon you had to be on the beach,' José said. 'Doctor Antignac will start the autopsy in an hour.'

After a brief inconsequential conversation, he replaced the receiver, pressed the buzzer.

Roldan entered.

'Grab a seat.'

He moved one of the chairs and set it in front of the desk.

'What was your first contact with Señor Sterne on the day he died?'

'He rang to say he would have breakfast at half past the hour.'

'Did he sound excited, worried, cheerful; did he say anything to suggest something was wrong?'

'He sounded as he always did, Inspector. Of course, he said no more than what he wanted to eat so it was very difficult to judge. When I was first employed, he told me he liked silence until after breakfast.'

'Did he eat in his bedroom?'

'He came downstairs. He did not eat breakfast in his room when he was on his own.'

'What did he do when he'd finished the meal?'

'Returned upstairs to bath and dress. He preferred to do things that way round.'

'What time would this have been?'

'I can only guess. Around eight thirty.'

'That early?'

'When on his own, the señor did not stay long in bed.'

An example of life's perversity. Because he could have rested for as long as he liked, he had not. 'What did he do after the meal?'

'Watched the news from England on television.'

'Where were his nephew and niece?'

'They had breakfast whilst he was watching.'

'And when they'd finished?'

'They drove off in the señor's small car.'

'How long were they away?'

'They returned later in the morning and were here for a short while.'

'Give me some times again.'

'Perhaps it was not long after nine when they left, just before midday when they returned for roughly a quarter of an hour.'

'This was before you found the señor.'

'That is correct.'

'They seem to be in and out of the house a lot.'

'The señor once told them . . .'

'Well?'

'They seemed to think they were staying in a hotel.'

'He was fed up with having them here?'

'It's possible. Once or twice, I did hear one or other of them arguing quite strongly with the señor.'

'Did you gather the reason for their doing so?'

'No.'

'How would you describe the relationship between him and them?'

'It had its ups and downs.'

'He would or wouldn't be sorry when they left?'

'Probably not.'

One seldom was sorry when guests left. 'That's it then. No doubt I'll need to speak to you again.'

Doctor Antignac, waiting impatiently in the ante-room, wore a surgical coat, a plastic cap on his head, a face mask which hung loose about his neck. His greeting was sharp. 'At long last!' He brought the mask up over his mouth, picked up a pair of surgical gloves from the table, strode briskly into the post-mortem room. Alvarez followed, far from briskly.

Because he tried to disassociate his mind from what was happening, did not look in the direction of the surgical table; he noted every sound and reluctantly deduced what it signified.

Antignac called out: 'Come over here, Inspector.'

He crossed the floor.

'I can find no cause of death,' Antignac said.

'But . . .'

'The damage to the head was of no significance. He did not suffer a heart attack. For a man of his age, his physical condition was good.'

'But something went wrong.'

'You imagine life cannot end as rapidly as it starts and as with little preparation? I conclude death was the result of vagal reflex because, despite a very thorough examination, no other possible cause of death has been revealed.'

'The lack proves what happened?'

'In the circumstances, "prove" is an incorrect word. One can seldom prove a negative. You understand the causes of vagal reflex?'

'I'm afraid not.'

'They are varied. The cause can be for instance, the disturbance of the glottis by a sudden rush of cold water, the intubation of medical apparatus, penetration of organs, abortion, dilation. A sudden shock, when in a highly charged emotional state and acute fear can have the same effect.'

'Would you think acute fear was the cause in this case?'

'With no indication of an alternative reason, that is likely.'

Alvarez feared injections. Did he now have to face the fact that the next time he had to have one, he might not survive?

'There is something to show you.' Antignac spoke to the mortuary assistant. 'Turn over, please.'

The body stripped of all clothing, lay on its back. As it was moved, Alvarez had the queasy impression something had fallen out.

'Note the circular areas on the shoulders, buttocks and calves,' Antignac said.

'They are significant?'

'Hypostasis – more commonly known as post-mortem lividity – sets in following death.

'Blood ceases to circulate and falls to the lowest parts of the body, producing purplish areas. This does not happen when pressure, such as clothing or contact with a firm surface, prevents the capillaries from filling with blood. So what do those areas tell you?'

The unspoken answer was, nothing.

'Immediately after his death, he was lying on his back.'

'He was in his car.'

'I am aware of where he was found. Nevertheless, he did not die in the car. The most likely place of death, considering the dust and dirt on the back of his shirt and trousers, could well be the floor of the garage.'

'That's impossible.'

'Unless the laws of gravity have suddenly altered, it is fact.'

Alvarez cursed gravity.

'Ana will be coming to supper,' Dolores said, as she put a mug of hot chocolate on the kitchen table.

'That's very soon,' Alvarez said.

'Why do you say that?'

'It doesn't give me time to arrange things.'

'There is no arrangement to be done by you. As expected by both Jaime and you, I will be left to do everything.'

'I'll try to make it . . .' Alvarez began.

'And will succeed.' She went across to a cupboard, returned with two ensaimadas on a plate.

'The case I'm on is exploding . . .'

'It may be blown over Puig Major, you will still be here when Ana arrives.'

'You don't understand . . .'

'I understand perfectly. Being a man, you lack the moral courage to face your shameful past.'

'She must be mixing me up with someone else.'

'You wish to accuse her of being promiscuous?'

'I'm not accusing her of anything.'

'Then you have no reason to fear meeting her.'

He pulled off a piece of ensaimada and ate.

He opened the bottom right-hand drawer of the desk in his office, brought out an unopened bottle of Fundador. After a second brandy, he found sufficient willpower to phone.

'Superior Chief Salas' office,' Àngela Torres said.

'Inspector Alvarez.'

'Wait.'

Had she gone into the army, she would very soon have been posted sergeant major.

As always, Salas did not waste time with a friendly greeting. 'Yes?'

'The post-mortem of Señor Sterne has taken place, señor.'

'Well?'

He was pleasantly surprised that Salas had not asked when it had taken place which would have highlighted his delay in reporting. 'Doctor Antignac found no cause for death and because of this has stated death was due to vagal inhibition. It means he may well have died from fear.'

'Obviously.'

'How much do you know about lividity, señor?'

'Not a question there is any need to ask.'

'The thing is, I hadn't fully understood what it could indicate.'

'Do not judge others by your inadequacies.'

'There were white patches on the back of the head, shoulders, buttocks and calves.'

'Has someone been able to persuade you to understand what that signifies?'

'The doctor reckons . . .' He hesitated, then in a rush of words, said: 'The señor lay on the ground for some time after his death.'

'After which, you are about to tell me, he climbed into the car and expired a second time with a coin in his mouth.'

'There wasn't one as far as I know.'

'That will be a very short distance. I was referring to Charon's fee.'

'I don't quite follow you.'

'I should be surprised if you did. Can you recall how you initially reported this case?'

'Señor Sterne had committed suicide in his car by gassing himself with the exhaust fumes. But even though that has been proved to be wrong, it was logical to believe it to be the case at the beginning.'

'That you believed it logical would have warned anyone but yourself that it was not. Did you then inform me he had not died from monoxide poisoning?'

'The garage and car were filled with exhaust fumes and he was slumped over the wheel. Of course, I am no expert in . . .'

'Very many things. I recall that you considered he had died from a heart attack whilst trying to open a door. The post-mortem negates that possibility?'

'Yes.'

'Then what is your present imaginative interpretation of events?'

'Some other person caused the señor to suffer such great fear that this resulted in his dying. Although his death may not have been intended, the law holds it to be murder. So it was made to look like suicide.'

'Your method of investigation would seem to be to pursue all probabilities and possibilities in the hope that when only one is left, you may be able to claim it to be the correct one.'

'I thought . . .'

'Have you taken more reasonable steps than that in order to make some progress?'

'I began to look through his papers to find out if they provided a possible cause for suicide.'

'"You began." You did not bother to finish?'

'At the time, there seemed no point when it became clear he had not committed suicide.'

'It will not have occurred to you that they might well offer a motive for his murder.'

'That is why I will return to them very soon. I have learned that he was wealthy.'

'To most, that would have been obvious.'

'A lifestyle doesn't necessarily indicate wealth, merely the art of finding the means to spend.'

'The one art in which you have some knowledge? Have you identified who are his heirs?'

'His will and other confidential papers are probably in the safe.'

'Have you thought to open it to confirm your judgement?'

'It is locked.'

'That surprises you?'

'I have made a quick search for the keys in all the usual places where they might be hidden and have not found them. So on my return, I will make a thorough search and if I fail to find them, will, with your permission, call in a locksmith.'

'Beyond that obvious step, have you planned the course of your investigation.'

'Not yet, señor.'

'A strangely honest answer.'

'I have only very recently been able to appreciate the need to do so because of the change in circumstances.'

'Circumstances do not change, it is the appreciation of them which does. Have you thought to consider why someone had cause to threaten him so violently, he died from shock?'

'He was not popular.'

'Why not?'

'He was rich.'

'You deem that cause for unpopularity?'

'In many cases, it is.'

'One must expect you to have a bitter view of success. Have you identified one or more persons who are known to have disliked him?'

'I haven't had time . . .'

'To do anything of relevance.'

'He was very friendly with the ladies.'

'You can be expected to show more interest in what you are doing.'

'If some of them are married, it immediately raises the possibility of a revengeful husband.'

'You imagine any married women succumbing to his lust?

It is beyond your comprehension to picture a wife who remains faithful, whatever the temptation?'

'These days, there are far fewer of them than before.'

'Only in a mind such as yours. You will ascertain who is the señor's heir, you will question the staff exhaustively, you will find out who visited the house on Monday morning, you will . . .'

As he listened, Alvarez stared through the window at the wall of the building on the other side of the road and wondered if the evening would prove to be even more exhausting.

FIVE

As Alvarez drove up to Ca'n Mortex, past the multi-coloured flower beds, a battered Seat Panda, driven by Roldan, came round the house quickly enough to drag the tyres along the gravel when braked sharply. Alvarez called out through the opened window – his car lacked air-conditioning – and Roldan left the Panda and came across.

'Are you in a hurry?' Alvarez asked. 'If not, I need to talk.'

'I'm on my way to the health centre. Susanna has just phoned to say she's ready to come home.'

His sympathy was immediate. 'I hope she's not ill?'

'Just a check-up. I'd be grateful if I might fetch her right away. I won't be long.'

'Of course.'

'Thank you, Inspector. I am most grateful. Marta will give you coffee and any help she can.'

Alvarez watched him return to the Panda, drive around his own car and away. There had still been a touch of deference in his manner. But then he was a Galician. And the unwelcome thought came to mind that there were occasions when someone might wrongly consider him to be slightly deferential to Salas.

Marta, wearing a black dress of angular cut, which emphasized the angularity of her appearance, opened the front door. He introduced himself since their first meeting had been so brief and was not surprised by her momentary uneasiness. Nothing could remind a person of his or her peccadilloes more sharply than a sudden meeting with the law. 'I wanted a word with your husband, but when he told me where he was going, I said I'd wait for him here.' How could Marta have sired a daughter of such beauty? It seemed to contradict livestock breeding where improvement came after mating quality to quality.

'That was kind of you.' She was more at ease. 'Please
come in.'

He followed her to the far end of the hall, through a doorway,
along a short passage and in to the staff sitting-room. 'Would
you like some coffee, Inspector?'

'I most certainly would.'

She hurried away, he sat, picked up the day's copy of *Ultima
Hora* from the small table by the side of the chair. The bad
news was in black headlines. The government intended to raise
the tax on alcohol. He put the paper down in case he also
learned it was to be rationed.

She returned with a tray on which were cup and saucer,
silver sugar bowl, teaspoon, jug of milk, and two icing sugar
dusted buns on a plate.

'I'd be grateful if you can find time to have a chat?' he said,
as she placed the tray by his side after moving the discarded
newspaper.

'I suppose so.' She sat.

'You are not having some coffee?'

'Never in the middle of the morning.'

He admired, but did not try to emulate, those who led an
ordered life. He took a bite out of one of the buns. 'Did you
cook these?'

'Yes.'

'They're delicious.'

She showed small pleasure at his compliment – perhaps,
like Dolores, she regarded it as no more than was her due;
alternatively, her thoughts were with her daughter. 'Have you
learned the señor did not commit suicide?'

'I've heard that said.'

'He was probably murdered.'

'Sweet Mary!'

He waited until she had overcome the shock before he said:
'Are the señor's son and daughter here?'

'They left after breakfast. They come and go all the time.'

'Then you can't be certain if they'll be back for lunch?'

'They'll phone if they want a meal here, unworried whether
I've the time to prepare anything.'

'Very thoughtless.'

'They do not consider others.'

'Tell me about the señor.'

'What is there to tell?'

'Your husband said he had few friends. Would you agree with that?'

'Yes.'

'Yet the señor did sometimes entertain.'

'Those who came here did so in order to eat and drink at his expense.'

'He was friendly with several women?'

'Yes.'

'I imagine you must have disapproved of his behaviour?'

'As any decent woman would.'

'How would you describe the women who stayed here? Pleasant, friendly, bitchy?'

'I was careful to have little to do with them.'

'Were some of them married?'

'It was not my job to know.'

'Yet some of them may have removed their rings and forgotten about the band of white skin around the fingers which never saw the sun.'

'Married women have stayed here.'

'Many?'

'Why do you ask?'

'If a husband learned about his wife's affair, he would have had every reason to have hated the señor.'

'Do foreigners worry about such things?'

'If a husband came here and accused the señor, there would have been a very angry row and threats made. Did that ever happen?'

She did not answer.

'I can understand your reluctance to talk about such matters, as was your husband, but I have to know.'

After a while, she said: 'There was a señor who came here and it was impossible not to understand there was trouble.'

'Was he married to one of the women who stayed here?'

'I cannot be certain.'

'His name?'

Once again, she paused before answering. 'Park or Parry; I cannot say which.'

'There was only this one occasion when there was a fierce row?'

'I remember no other.'

'I think you knew Janet.'

'She was not like the others.' Marta began to speak freely. 'She did not treat us as servants to be ignored; if we met, she always had a chat. Many times, she told me how much she enjoyed my cooking. None of the others said a word, even when I had taken endless trouble to serve a wonderful dish.'

Did cooks ever downgrade their own cooking? 'Was she married?'

'I thought not.'

'Your husband told me she was very fond of the señor.'

'Until he insulted her by having another woman when she returned to England for a while.'

'Was he very upset when she left him?'

'He scorned what he could take, demanded what he should not. She learned he'd enjoyed another woman's company while she was away and for her, unlike those others, love extended beyond the bed.'

He spoke slowly. 'I think I've asked all the questions I need to.' He looked at his watch. 'It's late and I can't wait any longer. Tell your husband I'll speak with him tomorrow. And I'll also have a word with the son and daughter.'

'If they are here.'

'Ask them to make certain they are.'

'You think they will listen?'

'Why not?'

'When you've met her, you will understand.'

He left.

What went up, had to come down; death followed life; the ecstasy of sliding into the sleep of a siesta, led to the pain of awakening.

He made his way downstairs. Dolores, her brow prickled

with sweat, was working at the stove. She spoke without looking round. 'You have not gone into hibernation, then.'

'I was exhausted.'

'You have done some work?'

He sat at the table. 'What are you cooking?'

'I am preparing Costelletes de porc amb salsa de magranes for supper.'

Seared pork chops in olive oil and pork dripping, diced onions, white wine, vinegar, cinnamon, seeds and pulp of pomegranates . . . 'It's one of your masterpieces.'

'It is unusual to receive such praise.'

'Why the special supper?'

Her tone sharpened. 'You need to ask?'

Clearly, his question had been inadvisable, but he could not fathom why.

She brought a wooden spoon out of the saucepan and put it down on the side of the gas ring. 'You have forgotten.' It was a statement, not a question.

'Just for the moment, I can't recall . . .'

'Does it cost you much effort to forget?'

'How do you mean?' He tried to change the conversation. 'Is there some cocoa?'

'Over there.' She pointed.

He crossed to the working surface, picked up the cup. 'It's cold.'

'It was hot when you would have come down had you intended to return to work on time.'

'Could you heat it for me?'

'You will do that for yourself or wait until I have finished what I am doing.'

'I'll wait.'

'Your exhaustion is so severe?' She opened the lid of another saucepan, inspected the contents, replaced the lid. 'You can bring me three avocados from the fruit rack since I need six halves as the children will be eating with us.'

'You are preparing a starter?'

'Aguacates con heuvas de salmón.'

'It's going to be a feast!'

'In the circumstances, you would expect me to serve garbanzos? You will wear a clean shirt, clean shorts, and polish your sandals.'

He was astonished. 'Maybe you would like me to wear a tie as well?'

'If you can recall how to knot it. As you are too exhausted to help me, I will get them.' She hurried across the kitchen, examined half a dozen avocados and chose three, put these on the table.

'You can move into the sitting room and leave me some room to work.'

'Are Ángel and Raquel coming here?'

'As my dear mother so often had reason to say, "A man will always forget when it suits him to do so." As I said this morning, Ana will be here for supper.'

'I don't think you did say . . .'

'I said.'

'Even though I don't know her, I've been looking forward to meeting the unknown lady from the past. Unfortunately . . .'

'You would rather eat the menu del dia at one of the cafés?'

Face Ana Loup or miss the banquet.

For the umpteenth time, he mentally tried to identify Ana. If he knew her maiden name, it might help. There was Ana who had jeered at his incompetence; Ana who had offered much and fulfilled her promise; Ana whose mother had been so old-fashioned she had made certain her daughter was never in his company without the presence of an interfering female relative . . .

The phone interrupted his unavailing search.

'Inspector Alvarez, Cuerpo . . .'

Salas said: 'I had been expecting to receive a report from you, having briefly forgotten that optimism is the enemy of reality.'

'Señor, I have been . . .'

'Finally, I instructed my secretary to phone you at the post. The call was not answered.'

'I was . . .'

'I suggested she used the mobile. She found yours was switched off, despite my order that all members of the Cuerpo were to keep theirs active when on duty.'

'Mine was on, but recently it has been behaving very erratically.'

'As one must expect with anything with which you have contact.'

'When I was out of the office, I was down in the port.'

'For what reason?'

'There have been several incidents of shoplifting there. I have tried to identify the man believed to be responsible, but without success.'

'You deemed that a matter of greater importance than your investigation into the death of Señor Sterne? It would not occur to you that any delay in solving this crime will enable the English press to repeat their canard that in Spain, only the siesta is pursued vigorously.'

'No officer would take a siesta when on duty, señor.'

'Being a hypocritical race, the English prefer to believe that perfidy when given the opportunity by the action, or lack of action, of an officer with little conception of the meaning of priority. Have you found time while pursuing shoplifters to learn who are the dead man's heirs?'

'The son and daughter had left Ca'n Mortex and so I could not ask if they knew where the keys of the safe were kept. I have questioned Marta.'

'I might find that information pertinent if I knew who she is.'

'The wife of Emilio Roldan who is . . .'

'I am well aware of his identity.'

'Marta confirmed that Señor Sterne had few friends even though many people came to his infrequent parties. As she put it, they were thirsty when it was free.'

'An indication of their character as well as of his.'

'That's what I thought.'

'Restrict your comments.'

'He entertained many women.'

'There is no need to indulge your unwelcome pleasure by repeating what you have already told me.'

'More than one was married and most were tarty.'

'Not an expression with which I am familiar.'

'Flashy, provocative, vulgar.'

'Pointless tautology. A woman who knowingly cuckolds her husband cannot be of any other character.'

'A little difficult to do so unknowingly.'

'An unnecessary vulgarity.'

'Since a married woman has a husband . . .'

'A witless remark.'

'A husband who has been betrayed has very good reason to hate the man responsible. There can be no surprise if he seeks revenge.'

'Must you repeatedly state the obvious?'

'I told Marta it was very possible Señor Sterne had been threatened by a husband and asked if this happened to her knowledge.'

'You expect her to be able to answer were it not in her knowledge?'

'She mentioned that a Park or Parry had come to Ca'n Mortex and had a fierce row with the señor.'

'She cannot say which of the two it was?'

'What two, señor?'

'You have the ability to render Cervantes unintelligible. Which of the two men had the row with Sterne?'

'There was just the one.'

'I find it easier to understand someone speaking Mallorquin, however barbaric a language that is, than to your speaking Castilian. You distinctly named two men.'

'They were alternative names for the same man.'

'So which did this woman choose?'

'She is uncertain which it was.'

'Does her husband corroborate the row?'

'I can't answer.'

'Because it has not occurred to you to ask him?'

'He had to leave in a hurry to fetch his daughter who was at the health centre. I said I'd return in the morning to talk to him and find out.'

'Would I be surprised to learn you had a reason for not waiting for his return?'

'Marta had no idea when he would be back. If many people are at the health centre, unless it is an emergency, one can wait a long time before one speaks to the doctor.'

'As one waits a long time, emergency or not, to receive a report from one's inspector.'

The line was closed.

SIX

Alvarez was reluctant to leave the office and return home. Even the prospect of the meal to come failed to invigorate him. Could he not revive his previous idea of asking a cabo to ring home and say he had had to drive to Cala Roig, Festo Valley, Parelona or somewhere far away? But he had to accept Dolores would not readily believe the cabo. Like all women, she automatically doubted what a man told her.

He made his way downstairs to his car which was in front of a no-parking sign, issued to that house by the town hall for a fee. He sat behind the wheel, lit a cigarette. He could claim illness and the need to retire to bed. It would be a pity falsely to cause her worry – she might have a sharp tongue, but was very concerned by the slightest trouble any of the family suffered. And, she would follow him upstairs to learn the symptoms of his sudden illness; being knowledgeable on what complaint produced what symptom, she would identify his deception.

Why was he so reluctant to meet Ana? Whatever had happened, they had both been young. Youth was permitted to make mistakes. But from the way in which Dolores was behaving, this had been no mere mistake.

There were times, thankfully rare, when a man must do what a man had to do. He drove to Carrer Conte Rossi, instinctively parked further from No. 8 than he need have done. He entered the entrada, heard Dolores speak, to be answered by a woman. Ana had not had to cancel her visit. Fate seldom offered support to those who needed it.

'You're late,' Dolores said. 'I began to think you had been held up.'

Her tone made it clear he had been wise to dismiss the idea of an emergency.

'Hullo, Enrique,' Ana said.

He returned the greeting. He had not deliberately tried to picture her – why try, when she was a mystery? – but into his mind had floated the impression that she would be around his age – although looking considerably older – have a round, characterless face with too much padding, lustreless eyes, grey hair, thin mouth, and stubby neck.

She smiled. 'Are you so surprised to see me again?'

However he judged his appearance, he had to accept she looked younger than he. Her features were pleasing; her black hair was carefully styled, her forehead, graceful, her dark brown eyes, lustrous, her mouth, full and even promising, her neck had Grecian grace. Her colourful dress outlined a figure many younger women would envy. Her appearance might cause some relief, but it in no way triggered his memory.

'No kiss of welcome?'

He crossed to where she sat, brushed her right cheek with his left one in traditional style.

'Time changes everything,' she said provocatively.

'I suppose . . .' He wasn't certain what he supposed.

'Would you like a drink before we eat?' Dolores asked.

Surprise delayed his affirmative reply. It was a long time, almost beyond recall, when Dolores had suggested he had a drink.

'I'll get it,' Jaime said, as he hurriedly came to his feet, an empty glass in his hand.

'Before you worry about anyone else, ask Ana if she would like another sherry,' Dolores said.

'I won't have one, thank you,' Ana said.

'Why not?' Jaime asked.

'Because she knows her own mind,' Dolores snapped.

'Two sherries couldn't harm . . .' Jaime stopped abruptly as Dolores glared at him.

'Did you know I was married?' Ana asked Alvarez.

'Dolores told me.'

'But before she did.'

He was trying to think what to answer, when she continued: 'I wonder if you would have come to my wedding with Emilio?'

'Why not?'

'You might have felt . . . But then, of course, a woman sometimes thinks differently from a man.'

'All the time,' Dolores pronounced.

He tried to identify an Emilio who would help place Ana when young.

Jaime handed a glass of wine to Alvarez, carefully concealing his own from Dolores' gaze.

'Dolores tells me you work for the Cuerpo,' Ana said. 'That really surprised me. You know why, of course?'

'Not really,' was his weak answer.

'You used to be so keen on farming. I can remember you telling me the maximum number of orange trees there should be in a hectare, how you would grow avocados because they would become popular – as they have – how almonds would need some form of mechanical harvesting to make them a truly profitable crop. All that enthusiasm and you join the police!'

'Without land, one can only be a labourer, and in those days . . . not so long ago . . . many labourers still had to share their living space with animals.'

'And you've never married.'

'Who'd want him?' Jaime asked.

'Must you judge others by yourself?' Dolores said sharply. 'I'm married.'

'You would like me to comment on that fact?'

'Would you still like to farm?' Ana asked.

'Perhaps,' Alvarez answered. 'But now one needs many hectares of land, workers demand so much money, a farmer has to have many machines which become ever more expensive. Long gone are the days when owning a hectare of reasonable land, working on it day and night, enabled a man to provide his wife and children with a bare living.'

'Yet perhaps your ambition hasn't entirely vanished? Dream on and one day maybe you will attain it.'

At Dolores' prompting, Alvarez had accompanied Ana to her car, a large Volvo.

'It's been such fun, Enrique, seeing you again. I wish I'd

learned long ago where you lived. I'm going to make certain
we meet again soon. Sweet dreams.' Her lips brushed his.

He watched her drive away, returned into the house.
Dolores was in the kitchen, Jaime was seated at the dining-
room table. He passed across the opened bottle of Marqués
de Riscal. 'You've landed yourself in the hundred euro
seats.'

'What's that supposed to mean?' Alvarez emptied the bottle
into his glass.

'She obviously likes you as much as when you were young
and likely teaching her it wasn't the storks.'

'You're talking nonsense.'

'I've got eyes and ears.'

'And nothing in-between when you go on like that.'

The second bottle of wine had not been opened. Since
Dolores was washing up, Jaime picked up the corkscrew.

She stepped through the bead curtain, a drying-up cloth in
her hand. 'Well?'

Jaime gently replaced the corkscrew on the table.

'She seems quite pleasant,' Alvarez remarked.

'That is all you have to say?'

'I suppose she's not bad-looking.'

'Being a man, you dwell on her physical features. You give
no heed, not one single thought, to her extraordinary spirit of
forgiveness. Had I been her, I would never have wished to
meet you again. Were I so unfortunate as to do so, I would
have made my feelings quickly known.'

'Yet she showed him so much warmth,' Jaime began, 'she
was as good as suggesting . . .'

'What?'

'I wasn't going to say what you thought I was.'

She looked at the table. 'Why is that bottle of wine in front
of you? You thought to open it and drink?'

'Of course not.'

'Then why was the corkscrew in your hand?'

He could find no answer, so said, pleadingly: 'We did have
only the one bottle during the meal and no coñac.'

'Since Ana drank so little, there was no need for you to
disgrace yourself by exhibiting your inability to drink

moderately. There is even less need now.' She returned to the kitchen.

Jaime spoke quietly, but bitterly. 'If you go on annoying Dolores because of what you say about Ana, she'll have us with empty glasses all the time.'

SEVEN

The front door of Ca'n Mortex was opened by Susanna. Alvarez greeted her, she muttered a reply. He noted her drawn features and reddened eyes which suggested recent crying. He wished a good morning, asked if her mother were there.

'No.'

'And your father?'

'In the village.'

Her speech lacked a Galician accent and possessed a Mallorquin rhythm, marking her years lived on the island. 'May I come in?'

She stepped to one side, he entered. For someone so artlessly beautiful, he thought, the world should be full of sunshine, not black clouds. Had a boyfriend been severely criticized by her parents or had one deserted her? The young could find life just as cruel as did their elders. He closed the front door to the usual creaks.

There was a call in English from one of the rooms. 'Who is it?'

Susanna did not answer.

A woman stepped into the hall. She stared at Alvarez. 'What do you want?'

Her voice matched her appearance. Tall, thin, a sharply featured face lined with discontent, a voice which proclaimed her inherent superiority. The English might have lost their empire, but foreigners remained lesser beings. 'I am Inspector Alvarez of the Cuerpo General de Policia, señorita,' he answered in English. 'You are Caroline Sterne?'

'Señorita Sterne. What is it this time?'

'I am here to speak to you.'

'I am far too upset to talk to anyone.'

'Naturally, and I regret having to explain that unless you

can tell me where are the keys to the safe in the library, I shall have to ask a locksmith to open it.'

'You will do no such thing.'

'I need to examine the contents of the safe.'

'You will not meddle with my father's private papers.'

'As I have tried to explain . . .'

'You will not touch the safe.'

'I need to explain that your father did not die in his car.'

'Have you the slightest idea what you're saying?'

'Yes, señorita.'

'Then it is your English which is ridiculous.'

'Neither did he die from exhaust fumes. The cause of his unfortunate death was not monoxide poisoning.'

'How dare you come here and talk arrant nonsense, making a mockery of our tragedy.'

'Had the cause of death been monoxide poisoning, his skin would have been coloured a bluish pink. It was not. Forensic evidence also shows that for a while after death, he lay on the ground before he was placed in the car.'

There was a shout from upstairs. 'Who's the visitor, sis?' A slightly built man came in sight at the head of the stairs. His long hair was groomed, reluctant moustache newly clipped; he wore a white shirt, overlong white shorts, knee-length white socks – he might have resembled a sahib of yore, had his features not been so weak.

She answered. 'He's a policeman of some sort.'

'Looks more like a local rag-and-bone merchant.' He chuckled at his own 'wit'. He began to descend.

Alvarez said, continuing in English: 'I am Inspector Alvarez, of the Cuerpo.'

Alec Sterne came to a sharp stop, his expression that of a man who had thought to pat a chihuahua and found himself facing a snarling Rottweiler. 'My God! You . . . you speak English.'

'I try to.'

'I thought you wouldn't . . . I was joking when I said . . .'

'A joke I might have enjoyed had I understood that is what it was.'

'Sis, I often make that kind of a joke, don't I?'

She ignored the question. 'He's saying the most ridiculous things, like father didn't die from car fumes or even in the car.'

'But he was in the car and the engine had been on.'

'You are Alec Sterne?' Alvarez asked.

'Señor Alec Sterne,' she snapped.

He remained nine stairs up, holding on to the banister as if for support.

'Your sister has explained what I have reluctantly had to tell her,' Alvarez said.

'But it can't be right.'

'The facts are as I have said. I am afraid both of you must understand the consequences of those facts. When your father died, he was lying on a flat, dirty surface. The probability is, this was the garage floor. Before rigor prevented this, your father was picked up and set behind the wheel of the car with the engine running. No doubt to simulate suicide.'

'What . . . What's it all mean?' Alec Sterne asked plaintively.

She answered. 'He's trying to say father was killed.'

'But that's . . . Can't he understand . . .'

'He finds it difficult to understand anything, so there is no point in telling him he's talking nonsense. All we can do is speak to someone who's reasonably intelligent.'

'Señorita,' Alvarez said, 'the facts will not change however hard you try to reject them.'

'Your ridiculous interpretation of them will.'

'As I mentioned earlier, I need to examine the contents of the safe. Would you please tell me if you know where the keys are?'

'No.'

He spoke to Alec. 'Can you tell me?'

'My brother will not do so,' she said loudly.

'Then I will have to ask a locksmith to force the safe.'

'I want the name of your superior so I can voice my bitter objection to this and to your attitude. Who is he?'

'I think I should explain . . .'

'His name?'

'It is unusual for a member of the general public . . .'

'I am not a member of the general public.'

'That would seem to be so.'

'You are insinuating?'

'I am agreeing.'

'If I thought you were trying to be insolent, I'd make damned certain you regretted it.'

'I don't doubt that.'

'Will you tell me who your superior is.'

'Superior Chief Salas.'

'His phone number.'

He gave it.

'I shall make it clear what I think of your attitude and your attempt to insert yourself into family matters.'

She made her way upstairs, followed by her brother.

Alvarez went into the garage, opened the outer doors to gain advantage of the sharp sunshine. The Jaguar was still in Palma, for a forensic examination of the interior, so he had a clear view of the floor. A careful visual search showed it was impossible to determine any impression of a body. He scraped up dust and dirt from the floor and put this in a plastic exhibit bag for forensic comparison with the dirt on the dead man's clothing.

Back in the hall, Susanna crossed in front of him, apparently unaware of his presence. Her expression remained one of bitter sadness. She went through a doorway to the side of the one into the garage. He hesitated, yet experience had taught him that words sometimes assuaged, however temporarily, bitter sadness. He followed her.

She sat at the table in the centre of the well-equipped kitchen. Tears dampened her cheeks. He stood near her. 'It is sad to see someone so very unhappy. Perhaps I could help?'

She shook her head.

'When I was your age, which is some time ago, I learned that however terrible things appeared to be, they will get better.'

She did not respond. He had to overcome the probability she resented him as yet one more hypocritical adult who could have no conception of how she suffered from having been spurned by her boyfriend. 'I was given a puppy, the weedy runt of a litter. We were poor and had little food, but I fed it with some of mine when my mother was not looking. I stole milk for it. Then it died. I still remember the pain when I looked down at its thin body before I buried it. Then, my father spent money he could not afford and came home with another puppy which was round and plump. It was with me wherever I went, hunted rats with me, lay near me in the field when I worked with my parents . . .'

The door opened. 'Why haven't you . . .' Caroline came to an abrupt stop when, far enough into the room, she saw Alvarez. 'Why are you still here?'

'Because I have not yet left, señorita.'

'You don't seem to realize to whom you are speaking.'

'That is obvious.'

'Are you trying to be insolent again?'

'That is for you to judge.'

'Leave this house.'

'When I am ready to do so.'

'Now!'

'Only after I have spoken to Susanna.'

Infuriated by his refusal to show respectful subservience, she left, slamming the door behind herself.

'No one's ever spoken to her like that,' Susanna said, with a trace of awe.

'Then she's been very lucky.' His reception of Caroline had momentarily banished Susanna's sorrow far more successfully than had his fable.

'She's a real . . .'

'Bitch?'

'I wouldn't dare say so.'

'You'd be superhuman not to do so under your breath. I have to ask you some questions, but I won't bother you now. There's tomorrow.'

Her brief relaxation ceased. A tear formed on her right eyelid. At her age, desertion by a boyfriend abolished the real world.

Alvarez climbed the stairs, paused to mop the sweat from his face, entered his office and sat. He switched on the fan. It was early July, yet already the heat was as great and energy-draining as if it were the middle of August.

He lit a cigarette. His thoughts were bleak. He could be certain Caroline Sterne would complain. She would vindictively make him seem to have been aggressive and uncouth. Would Salas try to defend a member of his command? Yes, if the name was not Alvarez. Then, probably, Salas would accept all he was told and would promise retribution. As inspector, his was the lowest rank in the Cuerpo so he couldn't be demoted. But he could be reported to the general who would have long since forgotten how graceless and rude a member of the public could be towards authority. In suitably grandiloquent terms, the general would declaim that there was no room in the Cuerpo for those who forgot that the public came first. Rudeness must be met with politeness, insult with quiet acceptance. Advice an archangel would find it difficult to follow. But as the infamous Don Alfredo had remarked, when told he had shot a man instead of the wild boar: A pity, but what's done, cannot be undone.

EIGHT

The phone rang as Alvarez was judging how much longer he must remain in the office before he returned home for lunch.

'The superior chief will speak to you,' Ángela Torres curtly said.

He reached down to the bottom right-hand drawer of the desk and brought out the bottle of Soberano and a glass.

'Alvarez, I have just received a phone call from Señorita Sterne,' Salas said.

He unscrewed the bottle.

'It was to complain about your manner.'

He poured himself a brandy which was generous even by his standards.

'The woman addressed me as if I were some subordinate. In the face of such ignorance, I was very tempted . . . Of no concern. She said you had been extremely insolent.'

'Señor, I may not have been as obsequiously polite as she wished . . .'

'A member of the Cuerpo is never obsequiously polite, nor is he beholden to a civilian's expectations.'

'I did refuse her demand to leave . . .'

'In robust terms?'

'She appeared to find them so.'

'Then you acted in a manner which can not be criticized.' The call was over.

Bewildered, but content, he drank. He had failed to mention the latest report from Forensic, but was not going to call back and do so. Only a fool kicked a bull when it was peacefully lying down.

He walked through the entrada. The sitting-room was empty; sounds from the kitchen meant Dolores was preparing lunch.

'Where's everyone?' he called out as he sat at the table.

'The children won't be back for lunch, Jaime has gone out to buy cigarettes.'

'It's a lovely day, not a cloud in the sky.'

'That is unusual for this time of the year?'

'Just thinking it's a great world.'

She parted the bead curtain to look at him. 'You have stopped at too many bars on your way home?'

'For the first time I can remember, I have been complimented by the superior chief.'

'Then has he been drinking unwisely?'

He put a glass and a bottle of Campo Viejo on the table, drew the cork, poured.

Jaime came through from the entrada, stared at the table. 'Can't be bothered to think of anyone else?'

'I didn't put out another glass because I've been told you've forsworn alcohol.'

'You're going soft in the head.' He went over to the sideboard, brought out a glass, sat. He started to fill the glass, stopped when it was only half filled and replaced the bottle on the table as Dolores came through the bead curtain.

'On Saturday evening,' she said, 'you will both be respectfully dressed.'

Jaime chuckled. 'We're to wear trousers?'

'Your humour comes from the bars you frequent.'

'What's it all about?'

'We are going out to supper.'

'Where?'

'Son Cascall.'

'So what's the menu? Roasted opium on toast?'

'You cannot avoid stupidity?'

'The name means the place grew opium poppies.'

'And you have to be reminded such poppies only produce a mild white juice which was watered down and used to soothe toothache?'

'Why are we going there?'

'We have been invited.'

'Why?'

'Because Ana has met you only the once.'

'She's only just been here.'

'Evidence of a growing friendship.'

'Or something.'

'Being a woman who considers others and is generous enough to accept their unwelcome habits, she will offer you more than one drink before the meal, more than one glass of wine with it, perhaps more than one coñac afterwards. You will refuse every second drink.'

'Would you prefer us to ask for milk?'

She returned to the kitchen.

Jaime spoke to Alvarez. 'The sooner she sees you tied up, the sooner we can return to living normally.'

Alvarez turned into the drive of Ca'n Mortex. A man and Susanna were standing by one of the flower beds. As he braked to a halt and opened the car door, she hurried to the house.

'José Marcial?' Alvarez asked.

'So they tell me,' he replied in Mallorquin.

'I'm Inspector Alvarez.'

'She told me.'

Alvarez watched Susanna disappear around the side of the house. 'It's sad to see someone so distressed. I tried to cheer her up and didn't have any luck. Boyfriend trouble I suppose?'

'Like as not.'

'The lad who's upset her must be a sod.'

'Weren't you a sod when you was young and got the chance?'

He was about to deny the possibility, remembered that it was possible Ana, despite her forgiveness, would agree.

Marcial knelt on a pad of thick foam, began to weed with a hand fork.

'You don't see many doing it like that,' Alvarez observed.

'I told the señor it was daft and would take for ever; I'd get the job done in a quarter of the time with a mattock. Told me then there wouldn't be a flower left at the end of the week. Wonder he didn't make me use this bloody thing at the back.'

'The back?'

'The vegetable garden.'

'Unusual for a foreigner to grow vegetables.'

'So you said before.'

'Knew what he wanted and was ready to pay for it.'

'And unlike me, didn't have to work for it.'

'Thinking of the women? I've been told a lot of them used to come here at different times.'

'He kept busy.'

'And some were married.'

'What's so odd about that?'

'Do you know any of them?'

'You think the likes of them would bother with me?'

'They might have had a chat about the garden.'

'Didn't come to talk cabbages.'

'How did you get on with the señor?'

'Did what he said even when he was talking balls.'

'Was he a friendly man?'

Marcial dug out a newly emerged wild olive shoot, growing from a seed borne by the wind from a distant tree.

'Did you like him?'

'Do you like the man who gives the orders?'

Not a question he was prepared to answer. 'You've been told he didn't die in the car; that someone put him in it to make it seem he committed suicide?'

'Evaristo said. Talking shit.'

'Fact. And whoever moved him was most likely responsible for his murder.'

'Can't think who'd want to do him in.'

'There'll be a husband or two.'

Marcial, the hand fork looking doll-size in his large, thick hand, stood.

'Going home since the señor isn't around to watch the time?'

'Easy to know what kind of a worker you are. Irrigating.'

'These beds?'

'The vegetables.'

'I'd like to see them, so I'll come with you.'

'Don't remember asking you to.'

They walked up to the house and around it on the right-hand side. Alvarez was amused, not annoyed by the other's curt rudeness. Marcial worked for a foreigner yet had lost none of his independence or contempt for authority.

Behind the house was a large kitchen garden and beyond

that a larger area in which grew orange, lemon, apricot and almond trees. A unique sight so close to the port.

Marcial went in to a garden shed; a moment later, half of the kitchen garden was sprayed with water from free-standing pipes. Alvarez remembered working with his parents in their small area of land, the produce of which had to shield them from the degradation of poverty. He had weeded with a mattock, heat evaporating sweat, arms and back aching; repaired the sides of the many irrigation channels drawn through the soil, which constantly threatened to crumble from the flow of water; controlling the flow from the deposito to each channel until that was full, opening the next channel and plugging the previous one with a clod of earth.

'Walking in the clouds?'

He started, not having heard Marcial approach. 'I was remembering how it used to be.'

'Before you just pressed a button? Money makes light of everything. It used to be the peasants doing the work, now it's machines.'

Alvarez pointed. 'I've not seen yellow tomatoes before.'

'Who had, until I was told to grow 'em and given the English seed.'

'Are they any good?'

'Eat one of them and you'll remember what tomatoes used to taste like.'

He waited for the offer, but it did not come.

'It's the same with most everything. Before it gets so hot, the peas are like you've never eaten 'em before.'

'An incomparable view to the front of the house, vegetable perfection to the rear. I'd call this Valhalla.'

'What's that?'

'A place of bliss for the souls of slain heroes. I learned about it from a Swedish lady.'

'Who slew who?'

'We'll forget her. Where were you midday Monday?'

'Having a chat with the King.'

'You want me to start wondering why you don't answer?'

'I was working. Same as I'll do now if you'll stop talking.'

'Gardening here or in the front?'

'Bit of both, likely.'

'You can be in two places at once?'

'Need to tell you I'm saying I don't remember exactly where I was?'

'Did you see the señor leave the house when you were working in the front?'

'No.'

'Did anyone else leave?'

'Them two.'

'The son and daughter? When was that?'

'Don't have a watch.'

'You'll know when it's time to stop work for your meal.'

'Me belly tells me that.'

'Did anyone arrive in the morning?'

'Them two came back.'

'When?'

'Not long after they'd gone.'

'Give me a time.'

'Midday.'

'No one else was around?'

'Only the car when I was leaving what came so bloody fast, I fell off the Mobylette trying to keep clear.'

'Who was driving?'

'You think they stopped and apologized?'

'A man or a woman?'

'Man, unless women want to be a bit more equal and have started growing moustaches.'

'Who else was in it?'

'Weren't no one.'

'You talked as if there was.'

'You don't listen straight.'

'And you didn't recognize the driver?'

'When I was tangled up with the Mobylette?'

'Did you recognize the car?'

'No.'

'Did you note the number?'

'You ain't been listening. You think I gave a shit what its number was?'

'What was its colour?'

'Black.'

'Saloon?'

'Hatchback.'

'Make?'

'Citröen.'

'Is there anything more you can tell me about it?'

'No . . . Hang on, there was one of them dangling things.'

'Meaning what?'

'You lot can't understand anything that ain't simple enough for a child. People hang up tiny figures on cord and they dangle around when the car's moving.'

'What was the figure?'

'Looked like a skeleton. Which is what the driver will be collecting if he goes on driving stupid.'

'How do you get on with the son and daughter in the house?'

Marcial shrugged his shoulders. 'Don't have anything much to do with them. But she's a real cow.'

'That's it, but I'll likely want a further word with you.'

'You get paid for wasting time?'

Alvarez discussed with himself whether to question those in the house. He decided that since they were foreigners, they would already be eating their meal. Much better not to interrupt that.

Dolores was standing by the side of the chair in which Jaime was seated; the television was on.

She looked round as Alvarez entered. 'You're back in good time.'

'I didn't want to upset things by arriving late.'

'Wouldn't matter so much.'

He sat. The programme was about maintaining health; eat carefully, drink frugally, give up smoking. A recipe for a hermit's life. She had said the meal would not have been harmed by a delay. That did not augur well unless the dish did not need much preparation or cooking. Heuvos au gratin? Eggs, spinach, béchamel sauce, salt, lemon, grated cheese, ham, olive oil, butter and tartaletas de hojaldre.

'You both understand?' she asked, as the programme finished and the credits rolled. 'To make certain you're fitter, from now on you'll have very little cream, butter and fat, no rich sauces and you'll eat only as much as you need, not as much as you want.'

'The woman looked like she's never had a decent meal in her life,' Jaime protested. 'So what does she know?'

'Much more than you, since she is an expert dietitian.'

'And also a sadist who wants people to suffer from anorexia,' Alvarez added.

'Typical! As Ana remarked, when mentioning that you carry extra weight, men cannot control their appetites.'

'Better a little extra weight than to be so skinny, ribs rest on the backbone.'

'That woman on the telly will lead a much better life since she will be the weight laid down in the table for a woman of her age, height and sex.'

'How much should I weigh for better . . .' Jaime stopped.

'You were going to ask?' she snapped.

'To have a better life expectancy.'

A weak answer, yet Alvarez was surprised Jaime had been able to provide any answer quickly.

'I will start preparing the meal.' She stood. 'Enrique, you will not have forgotten we are having supper with Ana on Saturday.'

'I'm not being given the chance to forget.'

'Aiyee! My dear mother was so right. A man is uneasy in the face of goodness.' Head held high, she walked into the kitchen.

Jaime drained his glass, heard sounds of movement from the kitchen, refilled it. 'What d'you reckon it'll be like?' he asked.

'We end the meal thirsty.'

'I mean, for us here. Is she going to start giving us meals which taste like hay just because you eat too much?'

'You eat just as much.'

'Ana didn't say it was me who was putting on weight. What with her and the woman on the telly . . . There's always someone trying to bugger up one's life.'

When Alvarez arrived at Ca'n Mortex, Amengual, the locksmith, was waiting in his car.

'Refused to let me in,' Amengual complained, as he shook hands.

'The staff did?'

'A manservant opened the door, I told him why I was here, he asked me inside. Next thing, a woman appeared and acted like she thought I'd crawled through a sewer. I tried to explain, but she wasn't having any of it. Even speaking in English, she made it obvious I was to sod off.'

'She has not affinity with us local yokels. We'll go in and beard the vixen in her earth.'

As they approached the door, it was opened by Roldan. 'Good morning, Inspector. How may I help you?'

'By standing to one side so we can come in.'

'Unfortunately, the señorita has ordered that on no account will you and anyone with you, enter the house.'

'We are about to prove her wrong.'

They had been in the hall for seconds only before Caroline came out of the green sitting-room. She faced Alvarez. 'You are unable to understand that you will not enter this house.'

'I understand that is what you have said.'

'Then leave immediately.'

'No, señorita, we will not.'

'My God! Who the hell do you think you are?'

'As you may remember, an inspector in the Cuerpo.'

'If you don't leave, I'll call the police to remove you.'

'That will be rather a stupid thing to do.'

'You become ever more insulting.'

'The police will accept my orders, not yours, which will make you look rather less authoritative than you probably wish.'

'I shall report you again.'

'As you wish.'

'The name of your superior?'

'You should have it since you have previously phoned him.'

'I want the name of his superior, who might have the ability to understand my complaint.'

'I fear that in Spain, complaints have, as we say, to proceed up the ladder. We will now go up to the library where we will open the safe.'

She turned, strode over to the green sitting-room, went in, slammed the door shut behind herself.

'What was she on about?' Amengual, who spoke no English, asked.

'It annoyed her when I told her we were entering the house whatever she said.'

'She reminds me of Jimena of the Sección Femenina.'

'Here's hoping the likeness is only skin deep.' A heroine to some, an example of pitiless hatred to others. Photographs showed her to have been attractive. A noted member of the women's branch of the Falange, she had been raped during the Civil War by a Republican corporal. At the end of the war, she had spent eighteen months searching before she found him. He had been grateful to die.

They went up the stairs and into the library. Amengual examined the safe. 'This won't take long. Doesn't need much more than a can opener.'

Alvarez sat behind the desk and hoped it was ridiculous to fear Dolores would forgo the pleasure of good cooking in the name of their health. His mind drifted. Tomorrow was Saturday. Salas would expect him to work throughout the weekend, which was irrational when the case concerned a foreigner . . .

'It's all yours.'

Amengual's voice jerked him fully awake. The interior of the safe was divided by a shelf. On the top one were a number of miscellaneous objects – passport, a clip of fifty euro notes, cheque books, residencia, tax papers; on the bottom shelf, bank statements, account books and several velvet covered jewel boxes.

'I'll get moving,' Amengual said. 'If I'm very quiet, maybe I can escape unscathed.' He left.

Alvarez brought the bank statements out of the safe and put them on the desk. They were from three banks in different countries and in each was deposited at least a four-figure sum. An annual income of between sixty and seventy thousand pounds. Perhaps Sterne had not seen that as real wealth, but an inspector did. Land, pigs, sheep, machinery to make light of work which had previously strained muscles, injured backs, provoked exhaustion . . . Did Ana really own many hectares of good land? Or had that been female exaggeration. Women could never handle figures; numerical figures. Had Jaime been serious when he had claimed she looked at him with more favour than one could possibly expect after what had happened when she was young? Whatever that had been?

He returned to work. In Sterne's will, small sums were left to those in his employ at the time of his death, ten thousand euros to Janet Nast, 14, Carrer Sam Miguel, Porto Cristo. The missing Janet? Sterne had had to accept he had betrayed her, so had been trying to salve his soul with money. Or perhaps he had merely forgotten to strike her out of his will. The remainder of his estate was left to his children.

There were two legal documents. The first detailed a trust fund. During his lifetime, Keith Sterne was to receive the income from the invested capital. At his death, that capital was to pass to named charities.

Had Alec and Caroline Sterne known their father's income would die with him; that their inheritance would be much less than they must have expected? However, Ca'n Mortex was a valuable property and despite the general drop in value of properties, must still be worth many hundreds of thousands of euros.

The second document was a policy issued by The Diamond Assurance Company. Sterne's life was insured for five hundred thousand pounds. Designated beneficiaries were Alec and Caroline Sterne. At the end of all the mumbo-jumbo, thought necessary in any contract, was a list of occupations and situations which would invalidate the policy. Suicide was the last listed.

NINE

'Señor,' Alvarez began, 'the locksmith has . . .'

'Opened the safe. A fact which should have been reported to me immediately, not when you choose.'

'How did you know he had?'

'Because I have been informed by Señorita Sterne that you thrust your way into her house, despite her objections, and that you insulted her.'

'She was extremely rude to me.'

'No doubt with good reason. She demanded to know the name of my superior so that her complaint would be properly dealt with. It took very considerable skill and patience to explain I was competent to deal with the matter and there was no need for her complaint to be taken further.'

It was clear Salas had not defended him; equally clear Salas' concern had been himself. Yet in the wild, even a cur would defend its own.

'Have you nothing to say?'

'I am not certain there is anything.'

'In the circumstances, I agree. Your behaviour was inexcusable; sufficiently serious for you to appear before a disciplinary committee.'

'I fear I will have to defend myself, reluctantly, by referring to the previous occasion.'

'To what are you referring?'

'When you approved my having been forthright when speaking to the señorita. If I can remember correctly, you hoped I had been very rude to her.'

'If you put as much effort into your work as you do in trying to avoid recriminations . . . Since I have persuaded the señorita there is no need to complain to any higher authority, this matter can be dealt with in a manner advantageous to the reputation of the Cuerpo. I accept it is objectionable to face a woman crudely trying to sound of some importance, so I

have decided there is no need to refer your actions to my
comisario.'

'That will save a lot of trouble, señor.'

'I am concerned only with the name of the Cuerpo.
Presumably, you have finally phoned me in order to report on
the contents of the safe. Or is that being too optimistic?'

'When one observed the wealthy manner in which Señor
Sterne lived, it seemed his son and daughter must have had
hopes of inheriting a fortune. That had to make them suspects.
Yet one needs to know whether he ever told them the truth
concerning the source of his income and the terms of his will.'

'Well?'

'I do not yet know the answers.'

'Why not?'

'There has not been time to question them.'

'You have reduced your working day to a couple of hours?'

'I have been at the house, sorting through all the papers in
the safe, and as there were very many of them . . .'

'Have you uncovered anything relevant?'

'Señor Sterne held an assurance on his life for five hundred
thousand pounds. The son and daughter are named beneficiaries. This provides a motive . . .'

'You are unaware that suicide renders a life assurance null
and void?'

'Naturally I knew that, señor. And the exclusion clause in
the policy specifically confirms the fact.'

'Then it has not occurred to you that it is ridiculous to
consider the possibility they murdered their father, then tried
to set evidence to imply the cause of death was suicide?'

'I'm not certain.'

'That is unsurprising, but depressing.'

'As you have learned from experience, the señorita has a
sharp character.'

'You will refrain from informing me what I do or don't
know.'

'She could be certain that his death, other than from normal
causes, was bound to place her and her brother under suspicion.
So what if she decided on a double bluff? They would set up
an apparent suicide, knowing the falsity of this would become

apparent to a medical man. That would seem to exclude them from complicity.'

'It is unlikely that however sharp, her mind can equal yours for irrational complexity.'

'I will question the señorita over that possibility. I have the address of Janet Nast, if she hasn't recently moved. She is the woman of whom Señor Sterne seemed to have been very fond.'

'You refuse to see the contradiction in suggesting he was fond of her when in her absence he had a relationship with another woman?'

'Love and sex don't necessarily go together.'

'You speak from regrettable experience?'

'Señor Sterne has left Janet Nast ten thousand euros.'

'Why?'

'I don't think one would expect an explanation in his will. But clearly it provides her with a motive for his death.'

'You have not considered the virtual impossibility of a woman possessing the strength necessary to lift a dead man into a car?'

'Not all that long ago, on the television, a woman tore up telephone directories.'

'An indication of the unfortunate nature of your viewing, but no proof any woman could do so under supervising eyes. Is Janet Nast a woman of great strength?'

'I don't know.'

'Absurd of me to think you might have considered it necessary to judge.'

'I have only just learned her name and address from the will.'

'"Just" no doubt being as variable as time was for Einstein. You will question her at the conclusion of this conversation.'

'She lives in Porto Cristo.'

'That has moved and is no longer on the island?'

'It will take a very considerable time to drive there. The English eat much earlier than we do . . .'

'It is not up to you to consider their habits.'

'No, señor. But I can't see it matters if I leave the drive until tomorrow morning and now pursue the more likely productive questioning of the brother and sister concerning their knowledge of the señor's will and life assurance.'

'Then at the end of this call, you will question brother and sister and learn the extent of their knowledge. You will report back to me immediately.'

'If they're at home . . .'

'If they are not, you will wait there until they return.'

The call over, Alvarez acknowledged he had outflanked himself. Sister and brother might well be away until late nighttime. Had he abstained from finding reason not to drive to Porto Cristo and so miss the meal at home, he could have gone there and made certain he had a free evening.

For once, luck was with him. Roldan said: 'I will tell them you wish to speak to them.'

He entered the green sitting-room, returned. 'I have persuaded them it is necessary to see you.'

Alec Sterne sat on a chair, Caroline on the settee. By each was a small piecrust table on which was a flute and a small earthenware bowl full of crisps: additionally, on Alec's table was a cooler in which was a bottle of Bollinger.

'Your constant intrusions have become a damned nuisance,' was Caroline's greeting.

'Steady on, sis,' was her brother's comment.

'I have no intention of suffering silently.'

He picked up a glass and emptied it, brought the bottle out of the cooler and refilled it.

'You're on your own?' she asked sarcastically.

'Sorry.' He stood, refilled her glass.

The humblest peasant would have offered Alvarez a drink, even if it was cold water from a well.

'Are you going to stand there doing nothing?' she asked.

'Perhaps I may sit, señorita?'

'You think you are going to stay long enough to bother?'

'That depends on you and your brother.'

'If anything was permitted to depend on us, you'd be out of here bloody quickly.'

Alvarez crossed to a chair. She looked at her wristwatch. 'We leave in ten minutes.'

'Señorita, I have to speak to you and your brother. The sooner that is finished, the sooner you will be able to leave.'

'We will be leaving in ten minutes.'

'You will leave when I say you may.'

'I reported your insolence and bullying behaviour.' She picked up her glass. 'I was assured it would not happen again. A false assurance.'

'Señorita, why did you and your brother come to Ca'n Mortex?'

She did not answer.

'You did not understand the question?'

'I ignore insolent curiosity.'

Her brother spoke appealingly. 'Why not tell him? What can it matter? If you go on like you are now . . .' He turned to Alvarez. 'Inspector, we came to speak to our father and ask him to send our mother more money.'

'Did he agree to do so?'

'He kept saying . . . He went on and on trying to make out . . . It was so difficult . . .'

'Stop havering,' she snapped. 'It seems, Inspector, you are determined to delve into our private lives and we have no means of preventing this.'

'I am investigating your father's death . . .'

'And make that rudely obvious at every opportunity.'

'It is my duty to learn all relevant details, even when such facts might cause distress.'

'I doubt that has ever caused you the slightest problem.'

'I came here to ask questions in the comfort of your house rather than in the bleak interview room at the post. However, if you refuse to assist me, I will have to ask you to come there.'

'Does it give you pleasure to threaten us? Your one chance to treat us as equals?'

'Will you answer my questions now or later, at the post?'

'I suppose I'd better give you the satisfaction you so desire. My father married someone affectionate and loyal, so he had no understanding of her character. When she was forced to accept he was having affairs by the dozen, she should have divorced him, but he encouraged her not to, saying he hoped

she would forgive him and they could be together again – any
lie to prevent the courts awarding her part of his wealth. In
the end, he agreed to give her an allowance if she did not
apply for a divorce. Inflation, financial chaos, left her far from
well off. Then she fell seriously ill and needed private nursing.
My brother and I helped financially as far as we could, but it
wasn't enough. So we wrote to him, asking him to increase
the amount he sent her. He didn't reply. We phoned and each
time were told he was away. I was certain the staff were lying
at his orders, so we came out here to face him.'

With her inner steel sharpened. 'You spoke to him about
the problem?'

'That was why we came.'

'What was the result?'

'He promised he would increase the allowance when he
could afford to do so.'

'You did not accept that?'

'You think me naive? Living in this house in style, employing
staff, entertaining an endless succession of females? He could
easily have doubled her allowance.'

'How did you accept his refusal?'

'Told him he was a real bastard.'

'That upset him?'

'I hope so.'

'You did not regard him with much affection?'

'In the circumstances, would you expect me to have done?'

'Then for you, his death was not a tragic loss?'

'No loss at all.'

'Sis!' Alec Sterne said wildly.

'Did you shed a single tear?'

'You can't say I wasn't very upset.'

Alvarez noted the quick look his sister gave him – contempt.
'Did you know your father's income came from a considerable
trust fund?'

'Our mother told us after he left her.'

'Did she explain the details of the trust?'

'She said we could not expect to be wealthy after his death
since the capital passed to charity.'

'Do you know the contents of his will?'

'Unlike our mother, he was secretive about money.'

'I am sorry to tell you that she is not mentioned in his will.'

'True to form!' she said bitterly.

'Small sums are left to his staff, a considerably larger sum to a named woman, the rest of his estate to you two.'

'Will it come to much?' Alec asked.

'Will it let us help our mother?' she corrected.

'There can be little doubt. This house and grounds are valuable assets. Should you wish to sell, they will bring a large sum, despite the state of the market. There is money deposited in several banks. Finally, there is a life assurance in which you both are named as beneficiaries.'

'He must have thought he'd live for ever or he wouldn't have mentioned us.'

'You are his children.'

'You think that stirred his emotions?'

'Did you know he had a life assurance?'

'No.'

'The sum involved is five hundred thousand pounds.'

'That's what we'll get?' Alec asked.

'Hasn't the inspector just said so,' she snapped. She spoke to Alvarez. 'Do you intend to bore us with any more questions?'

'A few. Do you know a lady named Janet Nast?'

'I met her for the first time a few days ago.'

'Where was that?'

'She came here to ask when the funeral would be. Tried to make out she was shocked by his death. Hoping to find he'd left her something for services rendered.'

'You knew there had been a relationship?'

'I didn't imagine they'd been whist partners.'

'Do you know if she is married?'

'She wore a wedding ring. My father preferred that. Gave him the added pleasure of cuckolding the husband. Why do you want to know about her? Is she the named woman in the will?'

'That is so.' He stood. 'Thank you for your help.'

Neither of them spoke or moved as he left. Roldan appeared to open the front door. 'Is everything all right, Inspector?'

'Is it ever?'

He walked over to his car, drove up to the gateway, waited for traffic to clear. Had Caroline been speaking from the heart when talking about her mother or from self-interest?

TEN

Seated behind his desk, receiver to ear, Alvarez waited.

'Are you there?' Salas demanded.

'Yes, señor.'

'Then why the devil don't you say so?'

'I was told you would speak to me and so thought you'd make the first overture.'

'To The Perfect Fool? Why did you not phone me as I ordered?'

'I was just about to, señor.'

'I find it significant that when you fail to make a report and I ask why, your invariable answer is that you were just about to.'

'That has to be a coincidence.'

'For you, the arm of coincidence is of infinite length. Why has it taken you so long to prepare yourself "just about to ring" when I said you were to do so immediately on your return from Ca'n Mortex?'

'I had to wait a long time for the brother and sister to return.'

'And you were content to stay there, rather than telling the staff to inform you when they returned so that in the interval, you could carry out some of the work you have left undone?'

'You told me to wait until they did return.'

'If I tell you to swim to Dragonera, you will do so without thought?'

'I can't swim.'

'The things you can't do become legion. Did you remember why you were waiting for the return of the brother and sister, or by then had you forgotten the purpose of your visit?'

'I spoke mainly to Señorita Caroline. They came to the island to ask their father to make a bigger allowance to their mother. He claimed he was unable to do so, lacking sufficient money. The stupidity of that was obvious when he lived expensively in a house which is worth a great deal of money since it is in a prime position, overlooking the bay and one can see the open sea through the headlands . . .'

'Presumably, you mean between them. When I want a description of the physical features, I will ask someone who can present them accurately.'

'They did know the terms of the trust fund and that they would gain no benefit from it on the death of their father. So that no longer provides a motive.'

'You have proof they were unaware of the terms?'

'I don't know how one could have proof of that negative, señor.'

'Nor do I.'

'Then I can't understand why you asked.'

'In a vain attempt to remind you that, lacking such proof, the motive remains.'

'I am convinced they were not lying.'

'Then continue on the assumption that they were.'

'They were unaware of the contents of the señor's will.'

'I need to repeat the question I asked a moment ago?'

'When I told them about the life assurance, Alec Sterne asked me, with some concern, whether he and his sister would receive the assured amount. That was significant.'

'Why?'

'It showed he thought there could be doubt that they would qualify, due to the staged suicide. Of course, any life assurance must make certain suicide renders a policy null and void. But it is fact that when someone is unexpectedly told he is coming into a large sum of money, his immediate reaction is likely to be to gain confidence that it is true and not subject to any proviso.

'And one has to return to the question, how could one or other of them become involved in the attempt to make it look like suicide since that would negate the assurance?'

'Have either of them medical knowledge?'

'I can't say.'

'Because it would have needed the ability to view matters with logical intelligence and imagination. Have you anything to add to your report which will not further obfuscate what, if any, conclusion you have come to?'

'No, señor.'

'Then you will question the woman in Porto Cristo. Do not waste any more of my time by explaining you will arrive there too early or too late, so would it not be better to leave the visit until another time.'

'I had no intention of doing so.'

'A lie is acceptable only when it is believable. You will not report immediately on your return, since I have to attend a lecture. You will do so on Saturday morning.'

Close to Porto Cristo were the Coves del Drac, known for centuries before they were explored and developed by a man who bought the surrounding land to their entrance and therefore the right to them, however far they stretched underground. The port was where the Republicans had landed and attempted to win back the island. The sea swept into the curling fiord where, as in so many ports, fishing boats had largely been replaced by yachts and motor cruisers.

The block of flats in Carrer Son Miguel had, unusually, been designed and built with an appreciation of the setting. The four-storey building stood back from and above the retaining stone wall of varying heights, at the base of which was a jumble of rocks.

Alvarez stepped out of his car and, shielding his eyes from the sun, enjoyed the beauty of the scene (less than that of Llueso Bay). He climbed steps into the building's entrance, pressed the call button for flat 8. The speaker buzzed.

'Señora Nast?'

'Yes.'

The single word betrayed her as a foreigner. He switched to English. 'Is your husband present?' If he were, she would try to falsify her evidence.

'You wish to speak to him?'

'And you, señora.'

'He is not here, but come on up.'

There was a buzz from the door lock. He entered. A lift took him to the fourth floor. The small square, on either side of which was a flat, was bare and one of two lights was not working. Flat 8 was to his right. The door was opened by a woman of his height, in her late twenties yet still enjoying the bloom of youth; her hair was jet black, her eyes a deep blue, her lips were sensuous, her colourful dress both concealed and revealed.

'I remind you of someone?' she asked.

She reminded him there were women who attracted without the intent. 'I'm sorry, señora. It is a fact that you resemble a cousin of mine.'

'I hope the memory is a pleasant one. Please come in.'

The small entrance provided a sharp difference from the larger space outside. It welcomed rather than repelled. The carpet was Persian in design, the large bunch of flowers on the small table was a circle of colour, the framed, colour photos of an English countryside provided calm beauty.

'We'll go into the sitting room.'

This was large, equally colourful, and through the picture window could be seen the fiord, the yachts and motor cruisers which represented a life of easy time and money he would never enjoy.

'Would you like a drink?' she asked.

A woman with manners. 'Thank you, señora.'

'What will you have?'

'A coñac with just ice, please.'

'Sit down and I'll get it.'

He sat. Beyond the headlands was a cruise liner, its super-structure so massive that in a high wind and truly rough sea, she must surely be in danger of rolling over and foundering. Not for him.

She returned with two glasses, handed him one. 'I hope it's right. But tell me if you'd like more brandy or more ice.'

'I'm sure it will be fine.'

'Then health, wealth and happiness.' She drank. 'I imagine you are here because of Keith's very unfortunate death?'

'Sadly, yes, señora.'

'It came as a nasty shock to read in the Bulletin what had happened.'

He judged her expression to be sadness rather than grief.

'Is it true someone killed him?'

'Yes.'

'And that's why you're here now?'

'I am asking many people to tell me what they can.'

'And you think I know something about his death?'

'Not directly, señora. But you may be able to help me as I understand you were a friend of his.'

She stared unseeingly at the wide window. 'He had a sense of humour, knew how to flatter a woman, made life sparkle.'

'You were a close friend of his?'

'A polite way of asking if I had an affair with him? Yes, I did.'

He was surprised by her immediate admission. To confirm his experience, she should have denied any impropriety until he explained he would have to question her in front of her husband and mention the evidence of the staff at Ca'n Mortex. Then he would have waited until she tearfully confessed.

She had judged his thoughts correctly. 'It's not all that unusual, Inspector.'

'I fear I must ask . . .'

'If Basil was aware?'

'He is your husband?'

'Yes.'

'I do have to know.'

'Because the knowledge might have so enraged him, he sought revenge?'

'There always has to be such a possibility.'

'Basil was well aware Keith and I were having an affair until I brought it to an end, just as I am aware he and Milly are presently enjoying one. We are adults and do not regard adultery to be of any account providing it does not distress one's partner. Indeed, it has the benefit of adding variety and the pleasure of knowing one is breaking one of the Ten Commandments.' She studied his face for a moment. 'You look a little . . . What shall I say, condemnatory? Is that because of the adultery or the cause of the extra pleasure?'

'Señora, you mistake criticism for . . .' For what?

'Jealousy?' She laughed. 'Drink up so I can refill both our glasses. Perhaps Basil will return before you have to leave and can confirm what I've said. I'd like you to meet him.'

He was not certain he could reciprocate the wish 'There are

a couple more questions I must ask and you may prefer to answer them when he is not here.'

'Obviously, you are still not at ease with our relationship.'

'The staff at Ca'n Mortex have told me Señor Sterne was fond of you.'

'As I was of him.'

'When you went away . . .'

'He shacked up with one of his tarts and she was careless enough for me to learn that. Would you have expected me to ignore such unfaithfulness?' She waited. '"But answer came there none."'

Because he had no idea how to answer her.

Dolores quartered a pear, skinned and removed the core of one quarter, ate. 'Ana phoned.'

'Someone else must pay her phone bills,' Jaime said.

She ignored him. 'She wanted to know if Enrique liked castañas since she wanted the cook to make soufflé de castaña; I said she needn't bother with a sweet since we seldom had one, but she wants Enrique to enjoy a really good meal.'

'What about me?' Jaime asked. 'I'd prefer something else.'

'Your wish is of no account in the circumstances.'

'What circumstances?' Alvarez demanded.

'Still trying to make out you don't know what's going on?' Jaime asked sarcastically.

'As far as I am concerned, nothing is going on.'

She finished the first quarter of pear, prepared another. 'I wonder if either of you has ever realized what is the biggest difference between a man and a woman?'

'I've a good idea,' Jaime said.

'A man lacks the courage willingly to admit to his past baseness, a woman possesses the magnanimity to forgive him.'

'That's all cock!'

'There are times when it is very difficult for a woman to feel in the slightest degree magnanimous.'

ELEVEN

Alvarez had not asked Dolores to make certain he awoke early since he had to get to the post in good time. In consequence, he overslept and when he finally arrived, the telephone was ringing.

'I expect my officers to be on duty at the correct time,' Salas said.

'Señor, had I . . .'

'Do not waste my time with meaningless excuses. Did you question Señora Nast?'

'Yes, very thoroughly.'

'But it was too much trouble to report to me?'

'You told me not to do so on my return to the post.'

'When working as intensively as I do, one is occasionally guilty of an injudicious mistake.'

'The señora freely admits she committed adultery with Señor Sterne until he betrayed her in her absence.'

'In the circumstances, the use of the word "betrayed" becomes an undesirable lens into your mind.'

'I am repeating what she said to me, señor. But I do agree with you . . .'

'It is not welcome to know that.'

'She was explaining how she views life. She was betraying her husband in one sense, but in another she wasn't because . . .'

'When a wife has congress with a man to whom she is not married, she is betraying her husband and no possible excuse can alter the fact.'

'But he knew what was going on. And he was enjoying his own bit of fun.'

'Your authority for so monstrous a possibility?'

'She told me.'

'And with your perverse interest aroused, you were unable to understand her lie was intended to make you dismiss her husband as a suspect.'

'Her husband returned as I was leaving. He was quite open about knowing of her affair and of his enjoying the favours of another woman.'

'A situation beyond civilized comprehension.'

'Neither of them believes there is anything immoral in a fresh partner from time to time. She added she gained additional pleasure from the sense of guilt which accompanies the breaking of moral and biblical codes of conduct.'

'The woman is evil.'

'She does have a different viewpoint from most, but if, as she said, it does no harm . . .'

'You seek an excuse on her behalf? Over the years I have become all too aware of your deplorable interest in matters which an upright man does not consider, yet I am utterly shocked to understand you can try to condone her behaviour.'

'Not condone, but explain. If one does believe that love and sex can be completely separated . . .'

'As you have previously and mistakenly attempted to suggest. In the past, the church would have faced you with the abominable heresy of your views. It is a pity it now has only moral strength with which to persuade conversion and repentance, instead of far sterner methods.' He cut the connection.

Alvarez braked as they approached the wooden name board on which was carved Son Cascall, turned on to the dirt track on which, over many years, small stones had been embedded to provide a surface that was solid and undisturbed by the heaviest rain. They passed an orange grove; the trees already carried recognizable oranges which evidenced good land. There was an extensive field in which was a large flock of recently shorn sheep and lambs, obviously healthy and well fed. There was a field – of at least nine hectares, he judged – in which grew tall, thick, dark green lucerne. This was farming on a scale only repeated once or twice on the island.

They rounded a bend and came in sight of the house. Large, rock built, it dated from the time when the strength to withstand burning heat and driving rain was far more important than appearance. Two kilometres further back were mountainous outposts of the Serra de Tramuntana.

'A palace!' Jaime exclaimed.

'A grand possessió.' Even Dolores, in the back seat, was impressed.

'Don Enrique!' Jaime said mockingly.

'A house that size is impractical,' Alvarez said.

Dolores immediately contradicted him. 'Nothing of the sort.'

'With rates having gone through the clouds, it must cost a fortune just to own it.'

'Houses in the countryside pay less rates than those in the village.'

'Not much less.'

'A great deal less.'

'It's a long way from the shops.'

'When have you done any shopping?'

'If one needs a doctor . . .'

'One drives to the medical centre or a doctor comes out if you are seriously ill.'

He braked to a stop in front of the house. Originally, it would have been owned by a man of great position and power. The labourers would have received small wages and if they complained, would have been sacked. There would have been little or no work elsewhere. In the basement there was possibly a cell where a troublemaker could be held. The course of justice would have depended on the owner, not the state.

'Are we going to sit here until lunch is over?' Jaime asked.

As they left the car, Ana came through the open doorway and across to them. She exchanged a cheek-kiss with Dolores, smiled at Jaime, asked Alvarez: 'Do we remember?' She kissed him on the lips. 'Let's go inside, out of the heat. I want to show you the estate, but that will have to wait until things become cooler. And anyway, Elena – my cook – says we must be ready to eat as soon as the meal is ready or it will be spoiled. One becomes a slave to one's staff.'

The entrada was large and its ceiling, high; the walls had been plastered and recently painted a light pink which avoided the sense of oppressiveness had they remained bare rock.

'I've carried out considerable modernization because in this

day and age, one doesn't want to live in discomfort just for
the sake of authenticity. But I've left one room as it was in
my grandfather's day. Would you like to see it?'

Dolores said they would.

Ana walked into a room to the left of the entrada. She
opened the shutters. 'I was born after my grandfather died,
but when I'm in here, I seem to know him.'

There was a large oil painting of an elderly man in fashion-
able clothes of the era and innumerable framed photographs
of men and women, most of whom looked uneasy. A pair of
hammer shotguns hung in crossed position on a wall. The
floor was tiled in island marble. The furniture was old-
fashioned, but not rustic since that would have suggested
'proper' chairs, tables and cupboards could not be afforded.
On the larger table were several silver ashtrays, traditional
presents at weddings and first communions.

'I come in here and sit,' Ana said, 'to enjoy the calm which
the past can provide. You'll understand that, Enrique.'

'Yes,' he answered.

'Like hell,' Jaime muttered, not loud enough for Ana to
hear, but Dolores' expression made it clear she had.

'Let's go through to the sitting room. And I expect you two
men would like a drink before we eat.'

The large room had two windows which had, with necessary
great care, been enlarged by removing stones from the wall.
Through them, the mountains were visible, their sides patched
with pine trees, their crests spearing the cloudless sky.

A middle-aged woman in maid's uniform entered.

'Please tell Juana what you would like?' Ana said.

They both chose brandy. They both were resentfully aware
Dolores was silently reminding then that they would refuse a
second drink.

'I do hope you enjoyed the meal?'

Dolores was lavish with her praise. 'I could not have cooked
a more delicious mejillones con salsa devinoto. And the soufflé
was heavenly light.'

Ana turned to Alvarez. 'Did you enjoy it as much as you
do your cousin's cooking?'

He faced a question that could not be answered. To praise Ana's meal at the expense of Dolores', or vice versa, was to arouse resentment in one of them. 'How can one compare perfections?'

'A silver tongue? So very dangerous to a young lady! Would you like to dine here again?'

'I certainly would.'

She smiled. 'You sounded as if you really meant that.'

They walked. Later, Dolores complained it had been for more kilometres than from the village to the port, she should have been warned to wear comfortable, not best shoes, and in the heat she would have found it far more preferable to remain in the house. Alvarez had enjoyed every moment. He asked Ana how many hectares she owned and she was not certain; he guessed the figure to be between a hundred and a hundred and fifty. The sheep were well conformed, the lambs filled with the energy of health. Not a fruit tree had shown signs of mould. All the crops were strong growing.

He was introduced to the farm manager. A long and varied conversation caused him to judge the other as intelligent, interested in his job, ready to accept modern techniques even when these contradicted the customs of centuries.

Jaime had jeeringly referred to him as Don Enrique. No matter how poor a man's background, married to the owner of Son Cascall, he would be given the respect of Don . . .

Dolores stopped by the bead curtain, turned. 'I'm only cooking a simple supper.'

'Why?' Jaime asked.

'Because if you ate as richly now as you did at lunch, your belly would blossom until you could no longer see your feet.'

'There's a joke . . .'

'Which you will not repeat. Enrique, did you enjoy the lunch?'

Alvarez, seated at the table, fiddled with his glass, half-filled with Viña Ardanza. 'It was almost as delicious as if you had cooked it.'

'You are right. There was the hint of a piquant flavour missing. Elena lacks the final skill of a first-class cook.'

'That's not what you told Ana,' Jaime said.

'I have to explain that a guest does not criticize her hostess's food . . .? Perhaps Ana should have tried to make certain Isabel got everything right.'

'Can Ana cook?' Alvarez asked.

'And why not? She may live a grand life, but she knows a man ceases to complain only when his stomach is full.'

'So why did her husband quit?' Jaime asked.

'Because like most men, he could not appreciate loyalty and the pleasure of giving rather than taking . . . Enrique, did you think there would be so much land?'

'I guessed there was a fair bit when she spoke of having a farm manager, but didn't expect quite so much. It must be one of the largest estates on the island. And the soil has a body as good as that around Mestara. It made me wonder if it would grow potatoes and strawberries profitably.'

'Did you ask the farm manager?'

'He reckoned it would, but strawberries are very labour intensive and there's not that much casual labour available around there. Potatoes aren't very profitable unless one can crop early and export to northern Europe.'

'Would you try to grow them if you had the chance?'

'I'd get seed potatoes from Scotland; strawberries, no. If pickers are in short supply, one can lose much of the crop. Again, the agents in Mestara would make certain we failed to get a good price.'

'"We",' Jaime said jeeringly.

'Just speaking generally.' But Alvarez realized he had been thinking as if he might have the right to make decisions.

It was Sunday, but Salas did not believe in accepting that as an excuse for relaxing. So it was advisable to go to the office and avoid any possible allegations of slackness.

The market forced him to park well away from the post. His route was through the old square and he was passing the abandoned stone-slabbed fish stall – all fish now had to be sold under cover – when he saw Susanna on a metal

seat, below the raised level. He walked to where she sat.
'Hullo.'

She looked up, her expression bitter. She muttered a
recognition.

'May I sit?'

She did not respond. He sat. 'I walked so much yesterday,
my legs feel as if they're about to go on strike.'

She was listlessly uninterested.

'Have you been busy?' he asked.

She shook her head.

'Do you help in the garden as well as in the house?'

She did not answer.

As he stared at the groups of drifting tourists, he tried to think
of something which might gain her interest. Two youngsters,
nibbling ice cream cornets, came to a stop and stared at her.
Certain their thoughts were lustful, he told them to clear off in
basic Mallorquin. 'Would you like an ice cream?' he asked.

Another shake of the head.

'Will you have a churros with me?'

'No. Thank you.'

It was unusual to hear a youngster offering thanks. Her
mother had taught her manners.

'Would you mind if I came back here to eat it?'

'No.'

He stood, elbowed a way between people to the large van,
the rear of which had been turned into a travelling kitchen. In
the back were two large containers filled with oil, heated by
calor gas. The air was filled with the hunger-inducing smell of
the twists of butter, sugar, flour, and egg, being dropped into
the boiling fat and retrieved crispy brown when they were
sprinkled with icing sugar.

The first churros he had known had been cooked in the
open, in a large battered, metal saucepan, the oil of poor
quality, heated by wood. He had demanded one. How old
had he been? Five, six? He could recall his grief when his
father had refused to buy him one. He had not understood
his father did not have even the few pesetas needed.

'If you're not buying, you're in the way,' one of the two
men inside the van said.

'Four churros.' He would offer Susanna two, despite her earlier refusal. He would eat her two as well if she did not change her mind.

A youth, long hair, stubbled chin, ill-dressed, was now sitting by Susanna and trying to engage her in conversation. 'Move,' Alvarez ordered.

'Get lost.'

'You want to come down to the post on a charge of loitering?'

'I ain't.'

'You will be when you're in a cell.'

The youth stood, slouched away, muttering words he lacked the courage to say aloud.

Alvarez said: 'I hope he was not bothering you?'

'Not really,' she answered.

One couldn't really blame the moth when the candle shone so brightly. 'I know you said you didn't want a churros, but I've brought you one – or two, if you can manage them.'

She shook her head.

'Try a nibble. When I'm feeling so gloomy that wine tastes like water, I eat something sweet to cheer myself up.'

'No.'

'You could eat a dozen and still be as graceful as a nymph.'

'You don't understand.'

'Susanna when my sky is black, I drive down to the bay to look at the water, hills, mountains, and their beauty is so magical, it turns my sky blue once more. Let me drive you down to the bay to find out if your sky changes colour.'

She stared down at the ground in front of herself. He had the sudden worry she might mistake his motive. 'Please don't think . . . I promise you I'm not trying . . . you know.'

'I couldn't think that of you.'

For the first time, there was an emotion other than grief in her voice.

He ate half a churros.

'Please take me there.'

There was a rubbish bin nearby. He threw the plastic bag, in which were the remaining churros, into it.

*   *   *

He parked on the grass verge with the car's bonnet pointing at the bay. The sky was a cloudless tent of blue, the breeze was too light to fill the sails of yachts which had optimistically left port, the sea was at peace, the sharp sunshine robbed the surrounding mountains of the air of intimidation they could possess when the sky was heavily overcast and the light poor.

Susanna spoke after a long silence. 'It . . . it almost works.'

TWELVE

Alvarez ignored the post which had earlier been left on his desk and tried to remember the alternative names Marta had mentioned as that of the man who had had a fierce row with Sterne not long before the latter's death. Park or . . .

He lit a cigarette. He had been surprised at the lack of vines at Son Cascall. Within a couple of kilometres was a farm which had been producing top quality dessert grapes for as long as could be remembered. The land might be very different in composition and quality, but it might not. One could grow two or three of the popular varieties of grapes to judge which was the best for the land and could eventually be a profitable crop. That would take a few years, but farming lived on time. The size of the estate provided its own problems. The sheep grazed much of the land, up to the slopes of the first mountains, and it must be a long and arduous job to check they were all well. If there were a large shed, sheep on the point of lambing could be held close to it and then taken inside so that the first days for sheep and lamb were not subject to the perils of sudden storms or unusual heat; illness could be spotted and treated before becoming potentially fatal.

He swore. Fantasy. Deceived into believing he might be in a position to farm Son Cascall. He had not married. Juana María's death had for a long while left him bewildered, resentful, bitter, unable to face a woman without comparing her, always to her disadvantage. Once his grief was controlled, if no less painful when he remembered too vividly, he had grown accustomed to freedom.

There probably were benefits to marriage. One always had cleaned, repaired clothes, a neat and tidy house with furniture polished, tiled floors mopped, windows cleaned; meals were cooked, the washing-up was done, and so on. But marriage had

developed disadvantages. Now, one's wife might consider herself
an equal, would think he should take his share in the running
of the house, would object to his having a little discreet fun on
the side . . .

He had confused himself with the thoughts of vines. He
tried to remember what he had been trying to remember . . . Park
or Parry. The names Marta had given him. He picked up the
telephone directory from the floor. If luck was with him, he
would find both men lived in the port or nearby. He was half
lucky. T. Park lived in Port Llueso at Guillem Torrenova, 44.
A Parry was not listed in those areas he checked. He phoned.

A woman said: 'Yes?'

'I should like to speak to Señor Park,' he said in English.

'Who's speaking?'

'Inspector Alvarez, Cuerpo General de Policia.'

'Oh!'

'I need to ask the señor if he knew Señor Sterne.'

'We both did, but . . . One moment.'

The wait was short. 'Tom Park speaking. You're asking if
we knew Keith Sterne. Yes, we did. Are you ringing because
of his death?'

'Yes, señor. I wish to know if you are able to help me learn
more about him. I should be grateful to have a word with you.'

'When?'

'As soon as is convenient.'

'What about now?'

He looked at his watch. It was not too late in the morning
for a trip to the port to interfere with lunch. 'That would be
very helpful.'

'Do you know the street where we live?'

'Yes.'

'We're next door to the bakers.'

'I will be with you in roughly twenty minutes.' He said
goodbye, replaced the receiver. The phone rang.

'The superior chief wishes to speak to you,' Ángela Torres
said in commanding style.

'I can't return the . . .' He cut short the childish retort.

'Return what?'

'I thought he wanted to ask about a written report.'

'I made no mention of that. There are times, Inspector, when I am forced to agree with Superior Chief Salas. It can be very difficult to make sense of what you say.'

'I suppose . . .' He had forgotten her habit of transferring a call without advising the caller.

'You suppose what?' Salas demanded.

'I was about to explain how one can be thinking so deeply . . .'

'A problem which will not bother you. Are you pursuing your investigation into the death of Señor Sterne?'

'Yes, señor.'

'I am reassured since there are times when I am not an optimist. What have you learned since the last time you managed to report?'

'I have identified Señor Park. You will remember Marta, a member of the staff at Ca'n Mortex . . .'

'Must you repeatedly confirm known facts?'

'You might not, with so much to do, have re-membered . . .'

'Cease using your memory as a yardstick for that of others.'

'I have phoned him. He admits to having known Señor Sterne.'

'You have questioned him?'

'I am about to.'

'You find no disadvantage in repeatedly offering the same excuse for your failure to carry out your work efficiently?'

'I was leaving here to question him when you phoned, señor.'

'A retrospective decision.'

'I don't quite understand.'

'Of course not. You have also questioned Señor Parry?'

'There has not yet been sufficient time to identify him.'

'You have been on holiday for the past days?'

'It took a while to identify Señor Parry . . . I mean, Park.'

'Is there any possibility of bringing order to your mind?'

'The names are so similar.'

'Similarity causes you to confuse lucidity with incompetency. You will make a report on your meeting with Parry as soon as it is completed.'

'Park, señor.'
Salas put the phone down.

Alvarez was able to park in front of the bakery to the annoyance of the driver of an oncoming car who had marked the
space for himself. The bakers arguably sold the best ensaimadas
in the port or village. Had Dolores bothered to learn to drive,
she could have come down in the mornings and bought a
couple for his breakfast.

He knocked on the door of No. 31, instead of stepping into
the entrada and calling out as he would have done had
Mallorquins lived there. The terrace, rock-built house, three
roads back from the front, faced a bar which advertised British
TV, especially football matches in the season. Local youths
favoured it. The Parks were either hard of hearing or not
wealthy enough to live somewhere quiet.

The door opened. 'Inspector Alvarez?'

'I am sorry to be a little later than I said I would be, señor.'

'Mallorquin timekeeping.' Park's broad smile stripped his
words of snarky criticism.

Forty to fifty years old, Alvarez judged, medium height,
reasonably well built, features of someone with a cheerful
nature.

What would have been the entrada was now the sitting room,
with comfortable chairs, newspapers and magazines on the
table, flat screen television, and a glass-fronted cabinet in
which were several small pieces of Lladro ceramics.

'May I offer you a drink or is that disallowed since you are
on duty?'

He had met this strange English provision before. 'That
would be very pleasant, señor.'

'Gin, whisky, brandy, lager or wine, red, white, rosado?'

'Coñac with just ice, please.'

'Shan't be a moment.'

After he left, Alvarez picked up a magazine proudly calling
itself the essence of the English countryside. The English pub?
About to open it and find out, he stopped as a woman entered.
Recalling another strange custom, he stood.

'I'm Leila, Tom's wife.'

'Enchanted to meet you, señora.' She had a pleasant face, but one which would not be readily recalled; she was dressed for comfort.

'Please sit again. Tom said you want to talk about Keith?'

'That is correct.'

'There's a suggestion he was killed. Forgive my asking, but is that so?'

'Yes, it is.'

'And you believe . . . Well, that Tom might know something about that?'

'Señora, at the moment I can believe nothing because there is so much I don't know. I am here because I have been told your husband visited Señor Sterne shortly before his death and so would like to ask him if he can tell me anything that might be of importance.'

'Recently? He can't have done.'

Park returned, carrying a tray on which were two glasses. 'What can't I have done?'

'Gone to Keith's place not long before he died.'

'Quite right. I didn't. And I've left your drink on the kitchen table because you said you were about to wash-up.'

'It can wait.'

Park sat, raised his glass. 'Cheers.'

Alvarez returned the greeting, drank. One of the cheaper coñacs, nevertheless a coñac. 'Señor, your wife asked me if Señor Sterne had been killed and I told her it was true. So I have to try to find who was guilty and need to know as much as possible about him from people who were friends of his.'

'I'd say we were acquaintances rather than friends.'

'The difference being what?'

'He was amusing, interesting, and could be good company. But it was easy to dislike him.'

'And did you?'

'One has to be younger than I and much more open-minded to accept his behaviour.'

'You are saying you did not admire him. Does that also mean you disliked him?'

'Let me put it this way. If we met in a shop, a café, we had a brief chat, but I never made an effort to see him.'

'Did you visit him last Monday?'

'No.'

'Where were you that morning?'

'Monday?' He thought. 'Friends were with us all day.'

'They had lunch with you?'

'Yes.'

'What did you have?'

'How d'you mean?'

'What did you eat at luncheon?'

'Nothing unusual. Leg of lamb, mint sauce, roast potatoes and chocolate mousse. Hang on. There was a starter. Avocado pears with oil and vinegar dressing.'

'What is the name of your friends?'

'Dunn.'

'Where do they live?'

'Lluchmajor.'

'May I have their address and telephone number?'

'I'm beginning to feel suspected of something.'

'It's my superior, señor. He has to know everything, even when of no consequence.'

'I'd better check their address because I can never remember the number of the flat.' He left the room, returned, an address book in his hand. 'Flat four, Titto Bosch, Lluchmajor.'

'And, if I may, their phone number?'

He gave it.

Alvarez left twenty minutes and a second drink later. Once seated in his car, he used the mobile phone to speak to Dunn. Having introduced himself, he explained the reason for his call.

'Señor, will you confirm you had lunch with Señor and Señora Park on that day?'

'Of course.'

'How long did you stay with them?'

'From the middle of the morning to the evening.'

'What did you eat at lunchtime?'

'A strange question!'

Alvarez did not offer an explanation.

'What did we have . . . Mary's a good cook . . . Avocados, leg of lamb and chocolate mousse.'

He thanked the other, rang off. He drove along the coast road, then halfway to Playa Neuva, turned inland. A kilometre from the bay, he stopped to study a herd of red sheep, a Mallorquin breed which had been saved from probable extinction by the enthusiasm of a few breeders and government subsidies. The Mallorquins had learned the need for conservation before it had become too late. Black vultures, a unique species of frog, foreshores, and woodlands, were protected; buildings of note were being repaired, rather than destroyed. Properties like Son Cascall were protected from development . . .

He was annoyed to find himself yet again considering the estate.

He had a pleasing siesta, overextended, as Dolores pointed out when he came downstairs.

'You are not returning to work?'

'What makes you think that?'

'The time.'

'I worked late this morning so was owed time.'

'You are no longer in credit.'

'Is there some hot chocolate?'

'I face endless work which must be finished, as does any woman who has a family who regard a wife, mother, or cousin as an unpaid skivvy. Yet, at your command, I am to make you hot chocolate?'

'It would be very kind of you.'

'As my mother observed, "A man's kindness is promoted by need."'

'Your mother and mine must have been of very different characters.'

'Why do you say that?'

'I can't remember my mother ever criticizing men in general.'

'She allowed herself to believe they had the right to sit at the head of the table.'

'That was the tradition.'

'In male eyes.'

He sat and watched her prepare the chocolate. Dolores'

mother was probably as responsible as anyone for the growth of the erroneous belief that women had equal rights to men.

Alvarez peeled a banana. 'I have to drive into Palma soon.' It was not something to relish with tourist buses and cars turning the autoroute into a will-he-won't-he speed up, slow down, turn, stop.

'I'll give you a list of what I want from that shop at the back of Jaime Three,' Dolores said.

'I won't have time for that sort of thing.'

'A pity. Then I shall have to go into Palma by train and won't be back in time to prepare lunch.'

Jaime said to Alvarez: 'Drive in a little early.'

'And get caught up in all the outgoing traffic when I'm leaving?'

Dolores' tone was sharp. 'You clearly would rather not help me.'

'I'd be happy to do what ever you wanted, if . . .'

'If you were willing.'

'I promise you . . .'

'Promises and pie crusts are made to be broken.'

'But what would the superior chief say if he learned I'd been shopping when I was supposed to be working?'

'The same as usual,' Jaime suggested.

'There is no need to bother you further,' she said sharply. 'I will go by train, however little I like being in one. Jaime will drive me to Mestara to catch it.'

'I'm very busy at the moment,' Jaime said.

'I will not spoil your exaggeration by asking, doing what? I should, had I thought, not expected either of you to find time to help me, even though my whole working day is spent helping you.'

'If it's going to cause so much fuss, I'll drive you to Mestara,' Jaime muttered.

'A gift unwillingly given is worthless.'

Jaime reached across the table for the bottle.

'There is no reason to drink any more,' she said.

'I'm thirsty.'

'There is water in the tap.'

'Every year, thousands more in the world die from drinking water than wine.'

'And you wish to lower the odds?'

Years of marriage, Alvarez thought, had not taught Jaime that openly to deny a woman's wishes was not a path to peace.

'What does foot rot mean?' Dolores asked.

'A pair of stinking feet,' Jaime answered.

She ignored him, faced Alvarez.

'I'm not certain how you mean,' he said.

'They have found foot rot in some of the sheep and what should they do?'

'Who has?' he asked, certain what the answer would be.

'Ana rang. She doesn't know what to do about it and is certain you will be able to tell her.'

'Female slyness,' Jaime said.

'You are unable to appreciate there are some who do not falsely pride themselves on being omniscient?'

'If her farm manager doesn't know what to do, he needs sacking. It's just her way of getting hold of Enrique and drawing the tentacles more tightly.'

'Your tongue betrays your mind. Enrique, I assured Ana that you would be in touch as soon as possible.'

'But that . . .' Alvarez began.

'Does not mean tomorrow.' She stood. 'You can clear everything and stack it neatly either in the washing-up machine or on the draining-board.'

'Why are you asking us to do that?' Jaime demanded.

'I have a headache and am going upstairs to lie down.'

'We haven't had coffee.'

'After great difficulty, I believe Enrique has learned how to switch on the machine.'

They watched her climb the stairs to go out of sight.

Alvarez brought the recently opened bottle of Felipe II out of the sideboard, poured himself a drink, passed the bottle. Jaime held his glass in one hand, the bottle in the other. 'I don't understand what's holding you up. Do you want it lined with diamonds?'

'You think only money counts? What about affection?'

'That's teenagers' nonsense. Go on like you are and Dolores will have us clearing the table after every meal.'

'You're making something out of nothing.'

'And you're making nothing out of something.'

There was a call from upstairs. 'Have you phoned her, Enrique?'

'I'm just about to.'

'One day you'll do something before you're just about to.'

He drank, went through to the kitchen, prepared the coffee machine. There was a mobile by the stove. He switched it on, dialled.

'What fun it is to hear from you,' Ana said.

'You're asking about foot rot in sheep. It's a virus which lives in the foot and on the ground, especially when that's damp. Very contagious, it needs to be treated immediately. A vet will provide the treatment, which must be very carefully followed. If possible, move the sheep off contaminated land once treatment is complete and plough it.'

'You know so much!'

'I worked on my father's smallholding when I was young and helped a nearby farmer who paid me a few pesetas.'

'Only a few?'

'Money was very short.'

'As it is for most. But some are lucky. Haven't you often wished you could be lucky?'

'Perhaps I will win the lottery.'

'There are other ways.'

'I must hurry off to work.'

'Dolores told me you couldn't hurry anywhere. Are you trying to get rid of me?'

'If I could, I'd carry on speaking to you for a long time yet.'

'Ever the gentleman! That's what first made me . . . I nearly said more than I meant to.'

'I have a very important case in hand.'

'It's wonderful to know you are there to make certain we can live peacefully. Do you see yourself as a knight in shining armour?'

'Not very often.'

'Other people will. But you haven't time to listen to me chatter when you're aching to get to work. So goodbye, sweet Enrique.'

He returned to the sitting room.

'Have you done the coffee?' Jaime asked.

'It's doing.'

'Who was that on the phone?'

'I phoned Ana to explain foot rot.'

'People get their kicks in odd ways.' He emptied his glass. 'If you don't pull yourself together and tell her she's the moon in your sky, you'll likely lose her.'

'I'm not trying to hold her.'

'Then even a headshrinker can't help you.'

There was a further call from upstairs. 'Have you phoned her?'

'I've just finished doing so.'

'Then you're on your way to look at her sheep?'

'No.'

'Why not?'

'She didn't ask me to.'

'And you lack the common sense to go? Aiyee! but the men in this house have minds of air.'

He waited, but there was no further criticism.

There had been clouds before sunrise, but these had vanished and the sunshine was strong; the tailback at the junction of the autoroute and the Ronda was longer than usual and Alvarez disliked other motorists who sat behind closed windows with air-conditioning units switched full on. Recently, he had had his car valued as a trade-in; to buy a new one would leave him exposed to being unable to visit a bar at will, virtually to have to give up smoking, and when there would not be a meal at home, to eating at a restaurant offering the menu del dia for as low as nine euros.

He swore. Comparisons were the arsenic of life. Life with Ana would be . . . She might seem to favour him, but there were women of theatrical nature who were free with affectionate flattery as a means of attracting attention.

A car's horn jerked him back to the present. He drove forward a few metres, stopped, drove, finally reached the Ronda where the traffic was moving with some regularity.

The underground car park was full, but the regular egress of vehicles meant he had only a fifteen-minute wait before driving down and finding a free parking space. He made his way up to street level. What had seemed proximity on the map proved to be a very considerable distance on the crowded, airless pavements. He had read in an English magazine that Palma was one of the most attractive towns in the Mediterranean and would not disagree with that, but he disliked it, as he did all cities, because of their lack of space, overflowing pavements on which people banged into one without a word of apology, roads which could not be crossed because of the relentless flow of traffic.

Parry lived on the top floor of the building and there was no lift. Alvarez arrived at the small, dimly lit landing, sweating freely. The door was opened by a man of his own height whose face lacked character, a fact accentuated by a despondent moustache and beard.

Alvarez introduced himself.

'What's wrong?' Parry spoke nervously.

An initial question he was constantly asked, often with aggression, whether the person was honest or dishonest – in the one case because of resentment, in the other, because of concern or fear. 'You have heard that sadly, Señor Sterne was killed a week ago?'

'Yes, but . . . You'd better come in.'

Alvarez stepped inside. The small hall was overburdened with furniture which drew attention, not because of its quality. 'I am here, señor, because I understand you knew him.'

'Only . . . Hardly at all.'

A woman entered from an inner room. Slightly taller than Parry, several years younger, her appearance, like the furniture, drew attention for the wrong reasons. Blonde hair was strag-gling in current "style", make-up had been generously applied, in particular, the brilliant red lipstick, her décolletage was sufficient to show she was braless, the hem of her skirt could be described as reduced to danger levels, and had the diamond on the brooch been genuine, she might have needed a bodyguard.

Parry mangled an introduction to his wife.

'What is going on?' she demanded.

'I'm not certain, my sweet. I mean, our visitor just said he was a policeman and . . .'

Alvarez cut short the inarticulate answer. 'I have come, señora, to ask a few questions.'

She regarded him with dislike. 'Why? Why do you want to learn something? Why do you interrupt?'

'Angel, he is a policeman,' Parry hurriedly said, disturbed by her aggressive manner.

'I have all the right papers which cost a fortune. In this country, it is pay, pay. What is wrong with them?'

'Señora, I am not concerned with such matters,' Alvarez answered.

'Then you do not need to be here.'

He could not identify her accent; it resembled none he had heard before from an English-speaking person. 'I am here because of the sad death of Señor Keith Sterne.'

'That . . .' She spoke briefly, staccato style.

The words meant nothing to him, but he had no doubt she was cursing Sterne. Then, to his astonishment, she produced a handkerchief and dabbed her eyes in a sign of grief.

'Inspector,' Parry said, 'we knew Keith, but we weren't close friends.'

'Because you were so stupid,' she said furiously.

'Angel, you know how things seemed to be.'

'I know nothing.'

'You were close friends?' Alvarez asked.

'Not really,' Parry answered.

'Yes,' she said.

Parry hurried to explain the discrepancy. 'I think "friends" does not mean the same thing in Hungarian as it does in English. I would say we were acquainted rather than friends.'

'That might suggest a reservation.'

'How d'you mean?'

'That you did not particularly like him.'

'We like him very much,' she said loudly.

'I have been told he was not a man one would quickly warm to. Would you agree with that, señor?'

'He could be very rude . . .'

'You talk sheet. I no longer hear beastly lies. I go to lie down.' She stamped out of the room.

Parry coughed. 'She is very upset by his death.'

'So I gather.'

'Hungarians seem to see things differently.'

'What things?'

'I just thought . . . Maybe if I had realized . . .'

'Señor, you had a violent row with Señor Sterne shortly before his death. . What was that about?'

Parry seemed to flinch. 'I . . . I never had a row with him.'

'It took place in the hall at Ca'n Mortex.'

'No!' Parry gripped the arms of the chair.

'One of the staff overheard you.'

'She . . . she's lying.'

'How do you know it was one of the female staff who heard and saw you, not the male?'

'I . . . I just said that . . .'

'She couldn't understand what the row was about because it was carried out in English, but she said both Señor Sterne and the second man were shouting. I asked her if she could name the second man. She said he had been to the house before and she thought his name was either Park or Parry. I have spoken to Señor Park and he was able to convince me it had not been he.'

There was a silence.

'It was you, señor, wasn't it?'

'No,' he muttered unconvincingly.

'It will not be difficult to learn the truth. I can arrange for the member of staff to see you and say whether you were the person arguing so heatedly with the señor.'

'You . . . you can't believe I had anything to do with his death.'

'Someone had reason to kill him, you had had a fierce row with him.'

'It . . . It had nothing to do with his death,' Parry said wildly. 'I swear it didn't.'

'You admit it was you at Ca'n Mortex?'

There was no answer.

'What was the row about?'

'Oh, God!' Parry bowed his head.

Alvarez suffered a sense of shame at browbeating so weak a man. Yet he had to continue until he knew the truth. 'Was it because he tried to become too friendly with your wife?'

'I . . . I need a drink.' He left in a hurry.

As time moved on, Alvarez began to fear Parry had pulled a runner, too afraid – or unwilling – to face any more questioning. Then he returned, a filled glass in his hand. He sat heavily. Whisky slopped over the rim of the glass and fell on his shorts.

'Was that the reason?' Alvarez asked again.

'I tried to tell her what kind of a man he was. She wouldn't listen. He could be very pleasant if he wanted to be. And to someone who'd been as poor as she had . . . She thought me rich when we first met after I'd written to the firm in the advertisement.'

'What advertisement?'

'It doesn't matter.'

'I need to decide. Please tell me.'

'It was in . . . Must you know?'

'Yes.'

'In the magazine at the hairdresser. I read it and thought . . . Later I bought the latest copy of the magazine and the advertisement was still in it and . . .'

He was slurring words. Alvarez was surprised how quickly the alcohol had affected him.

'They told me where to meet her at Dover. I was to tell the immigration people that I had invited her over for a holiday. They seemed a bit worried, perhaps it was the difference between us, but in the end, there was no trouble.

'We moved out here because my home had become worth quite a lot of money and I had always wanted to live where it would be warm. Then we went to a party. Keith was there. I wasn't going to bother to talk to him, knowing how contemptuously rude he'd be. But he came over and chatted. I guessed why.' He came to his feet, left.

He returned with a filled glass. 'He invited us on a trip to Menorca on his yacht. I didn't want to go, but Mónika was so thrilled, I agreed. The sea was very choppy and I was seasick and spent most of the time in a cabin. We were invited on another trip. I wouldn't go. I asked her not to, but she insisted. I had to return to England for a week and when I came back, a man I've always disliked remarked how Mónika had become a very keen sailor.'

'The row at Ca'n Mortex did concern your wife?'

He drank. 'I asked . . . I asked him not to keep seeing her. He jeered, said a man needed balls to keep a woman contented. I shouted he had the morals of an alley tom-cat. That enraged him.'

'It can be unpleasant to have one's character correctly described.'

'But it made him give her up. Or maybe that wasn't why he became friendly with another woman. Mónika was so angry when she understood. I tried to say it was for the best which just made her even more furious . . . I've not seen him since then. I swear I didn't kill him even though he'd damaged our life so much.'

It was impossible to believe Parry could have offered a threat sufficient to cause fatal fear, the quick wit to consider a fake suicide, or possessed the strength to lift the body into the car.

THIRTEEN

'Is it important?' Ángela Torres demanded. 'The superior chief is very busy.'

'I'll ring again later,' Alvarez hurriedly replied.

'However,' she continued, 'since he has been expecting to hear from you, you can wait until he is free.'

'I'm very busy and can't afford to waste time waiting.'

'Superior Chief Salas will be interested to learn it is a waste of time to wait to speak to him.'

'That's not what I meant.'

'It always helps, Inspector, to say what one means.'

When she had been appointed Salas' secretary, she had rightly acknowledged her lowly position. But, an eternal spinster, regarding her boss with concealed, undemanding affection, she had developed an authoritative character.

He sat back in the chair, raised his feet up on to the desk. The post-mortem had revealed no cause for Sterne's death, providing strong credence for the diagnosis of vagal inhibition. Caused by what? The impact of food or water on the glottis, sudden shock, extreme fear, internal stretching during an operation . . . He couldn't remember the other causes, but in this instance, they were unimportant.

Fear and shock. What had been the literally heart-stopping event? Who had threatened him so violently, he had believed he was about to be murdered? A cuckolded husband? A violent row over money? Enquiries had so far eliminated those who had been suspect. There would be many husbands who had reason to threaten him with violence, but how to identify them? And was there, amongst the ex-patriots who seemed to swap wives as freely as the name of the latest good restaurant, a husband who was concerned about his wife's behaviour?

Caroline and Alec Sterne, on their own account, had reason to dislike, probably hate their father. Caroline would have faced him with wildcat fury. But then would she have tried to fake his suicide, invalidating the assurance policy. Or had she not known that would automatically happen? A question he had asked himself before and reached the same answer as he did now. She was far too sharp not to know.

'Alvarez?' Salas spoke as if pronouncing sentence.

'Yes, señor.'

'Do you have a report to make or are you about to say you have yet to carry out the work necessary to make one?'

'I have questioned both Señors Parry and Park.'

'Did you succeed in addressing each by his correct name?'

'Yes, but it wouldn't have mattered if I hadn't.'

'You can see no disadvantage, no self-confessed ineptitude, in mistaking the name of the man you are addressing?'

'Had I spoken to Señor Park and called him Parry, he would have corrected me immediately.'

'This display of ignorance would not have embarrassed you?'

'Everyone sometimes mixes up names. Even you, señor, misnamed Parry for Park. Or was it the other way round?'

'A unique mistake, caused by your inability to speak lucidly. What have you to report?'

'Señor Park lives in Port Llueso. He knew Señor Sterne, had visited Ca'n Mortex, yet claimed to be an acquaintance, rather than a friend. He admitted he had argued with Sterne on occasions, but said he had done so only pleasantly.'

'A pleasant argument does not seem to you to be an oxymoron?'

'I am not certain of that. But if I say Ibiza is to the west of Mallorca, you may argue it is to the east . . .'

'It pleases you to suggest I am so ignorant?'

'I was not making any such suggestion, señor.'

'Telling me I would place Ibiza to the east most certainly does.'

'It was just postulating a possibility.'

'Which could only arise in a mind such as yours.'

'And I wasn't meaning you, señor.'

'Then why did you say "you"?'

'"You" was everyone. And the possible argument was hypothetical.'

'What argument?'

'The one you didn't have, but might have done had it been a friendly one.'

'You will start again and refrain from posing ridiculous situations. And you will not mention mice or wild elephants in Andalucia. Whom did you question?'

'Señors Park and Parry.'

'What did Park tell you?'

'Señor Sterne was an acquaintance rather than a friend. He had never had a row with him and had not visited Ca'n Mortex that Monday.'

'Perhaps you remembered to ask where he was in the middle of the day?'

'He and his wife had friends to lunch.'

'You have questioned the friends?'

'Yes.'

'At their home?'

'It didn't seem necessary to spend the time driving there.'

'They are experienced in telepathy and on the same channel as you?'

'I asked Señor Park what he had eaten for lunch that day. He told me, avocado pears, leg of lamb, and chocolate mousse.'

'Had he answered lobster, roast beef, and strawberries, you would have known he was lying?'

'I phoned Señora Dunn; rather, Señor Dunn . . .'

'You are having further trouble with identities?'

'The meal had been exactly as Señora Park had said.'

'You accepted that as confirming the alibi?'

'The Dunns could not have known what I was going to ask.'

'It seems you credit those concerned with an intelligence similar to yours. It would not occur to you the Dunns had told Park how to answer your questions?'

'My call was immediately after talking to Señor Dunn. Had Señor Park phoned the Dunns, I would have had an engaged signal. I got straight through.'

'You have spoken to Señor Parry?'

'I drove into Palma to do so.'

'Why?'

'That is where he lives.'

'My question was to remind you that you should have
mentioned the fact. Perhaps you were pleased to imagine I
might have forgotten such details.'

'Of course not, señor.'

'Do you intend to tell me what Señor Parry had to say?'

'He admitted a row with Señor Sterne. Clearly, that was the
row Marta mentioned. Marta is the wife of . . .'

'Who are her grandparents?'

'I . . . Is that important?'

'It is of supreme unimportance, but having provided me
with information of which I was cognizant, I thought you
might wish to add some of which I was not.'

'There are occasions when you blame me for not identifying
who I am talking about.'

'Eventually, did you remember to ask Parry what the row
was about?'

'Señor Sterne had been enjoying the favours of his wife.'

'To admit adultery is a favour to whom?'

'To Sterne. And since Parry was possibly not up to it, perhaps
voyeuristically to himself.'

'Your imagination invades the lower reaches of the Inferno.
Were the Inquisition extant, you would be examined on the
charge of possessing a corrupting influence. You will continue
your report without further unnecessary, salacious comment.'

'The facts would seem to mark Señor Parry as a strong
suspect, but he cannot be realistically considered as such. He
is incapable of killing a mouse. He has so negative a character,
is so lacking in self-confidence, it is astonishing he could even
bring himself to face Señor Sterne and demand that he leave
his wife alone.'

'You have not said whether he has afforded a valid alibi.'

'He hasn't because, as I have just explained, there really
was no need to press him to do so.'

'Your judgement, based on little but self-deception, is more
important than fact?'

'Señor, he's best described as being absent even when he's
there.'

'An unusual achievement.'

'He's so gormless, no woman would go out with him.

So when he read in an advertisement that a firm would introduce men to beautiful young Hungarian women, he decided
to get to know one.'

'You are talking about pen-pals?'

'Not exactly. It was to be a warm friendship.'

'A good friendship is a warm one.'

'"Warm" implied something more than friendship.'

'What exactly?'

'A sexual relationship.'

'It requires a mind such as yours to derive such meaning
from simple, honest words. It seems you have spent your time
pursuing matters of concern only to a man of your unfortunate
nature and as a consequence have failed to pursue the investigation with the slightest degree of competency. You will
question Parry again and ensure whether or not he can provide
a valid alibi.'

'Very well, señor. But I don't think a mouse ever attacks
a cat.'

'You have an unfortunate predilection for mice.'

The line was closed.

Alvarez leaned over and opened the bottom right-hand
drawer of the desk.

Dolores had cooked supper before she retired to bed, but
lacking the last tweaks she would have given – a little more
grated cheese, another half onion, the juice of another lemon
– Alvarez was disappointed by the dish.

After finishing his second helping, he emptied his glass,
refilled it from the bottle of Sangre de Toro. 'Had you better
go up and see if she needs anything?'

'She'll shout if she does,' Jaime replied.

'What's her trouble?'

'A headache or something. Woman trouble. They have them
all the time.'

'She seemed fit at lunchtime.'

'It's a funny thing about women, they shout equality, but they've
no staying power. If they had to work as hard as us, they'd
collapse.'

The phone rang. Each waited for the other to answer the call.

'Are you deaf?' came the shout from upstairs.

'Can't be much wrong with her,' Jaime muttered as he stood. He went through to the entrada, returned. 'It's for you.'

'Who is it?'

'Her.' Jaime sat.

'Ana?'

'Expecting Madonna?'

Alvarez went through to the entrada.

'Enrique. I hoped to have a word with you, but was expecting to talk to Dolores first.'

'Did Jaime tell you she's not too well?'

'No. Nothing serious, I hope?'

'Doesn't seem to be.'

'You don't know for sure? What would you do if I was ill? Sit by my bedside and read poems to me? But that's not your style! You'd tell me how this sheep is getting on with its broken leg, how that field of corn is looking.'

He wondered if she realized that she was inferring the sheep would be his concern because they were under his control.

'Of course, you wouldn't willingly sit by my bedside. Or is that wronging you? Most men do become so uneasy in a sick room. It reminds them that as strong as they think they are, illness can turn them into weaklings. Enough! Why are we so morbid? I'm happy. Are you?'

'Yes.'

'Not an enthusiastic answer. Is something wrong?'

'No.'

'Sounds more like a secret "yes". Are you troubled because you think you ought to tell me something which might disturb me?'

'I'm having problems at work and can't forget them even when I'm home.'

'So it's not that you . . . I was beginning to have horrid thoughts, but you've blown them away.'

Dispelled by his saying it was work which troubled him. Had she feared he was about to admit he would only be at her bedside as a friend?

'Where have you gone, Enrique?'

'I suddenly remembered something.'

'But not what you've failed to do at work, I'm certain. You are far too conscientious for that to happen. Perhaps you'd rather not admit where your thoughts had gone to, what with talk about bedside?' She laughed. 'Before I retire, will you do something for me?'

'If I can.'

'There is something you can't do? I'm sure there isn't. I see you slaying dragons with gusto.'

'My money would be on the dragon.'

She laughed again. 'Tell Dolores I wish her fit in no time. And a hundred thanks for the recipe. Don't drift away and forget to tell her that, will you?'

'I'll pass on the message immediately.'

'Then sweet dreams, dear Enrique.'

He returned to the other room. 'Do you know if Dolores is awake?'

'Judging by the way she shouted, she is,' Jaime said.

'There's a message for her from Ana.'

He went upstairs, knocked on the door of the bedroom, entered. Before he could ask her how she was, she said: 'Who was that?'

'Ana. She hopes you'll soon be very much better and thanks for the recipe.'

'Her cook must follow my instructions exactly and not think she knows better.'

'What recipe did she want?'

'Conejo con pimiento verdes.'

'One of my favourites.'

'Why else would she want to know how best to cook it.'

'But how . . . Did you tell her I liked it?'

'You ask foolish questions, I am feeling tired again, so you can leave.'

This was the second time she had given Ana one of his favourite dishes. He was hopelessly outgunned.

FOURTEEN

The drive into Palma was even more unwelcome than on the previous day. It was hotter, the roads were more crowded, the coach drivers more aggressive, the underground car-park was so busy he had to wait in a queue for twenty minutes before free to drive down into it.

Parry opened the front door of his flat, was shocked to face Alvarez.

'I'm sorry to bother you again, señor.'

'What . . . Why . . .?'

'The boss has said I must ask you one or two more questions. He'll find problems in heaven.' Alvarez waited, finally said: 'Do you mind if I come in?'

Parry stepped to one side. There was a call: 'Who is it?'

Mónika came into the hall as Parry shut the door. She stared at Alvarez. 'Why you come again?' She was dressed with an equal lack of taste and slightly more exposure. 'You are worrying us.'

'I have to speak to your husband.'

'He is taking me out.'

'Sweet,' Parry said hurriedly, 'I'm sure the inspector won't delay our trip.'

'We go now.'

'Please be reasonable.'

'You treat me like I am nobody.'

'You know that's not true.'

'You ignore me.' She left, entered a room, slammed the door shut.

'She . . . she can get upset when something unexpected happens,' Parry said nervously.

'I'm sorry to be the cause.'

'How can she expect me to know you were coming. I try my best to do what she wants, but sometimes it's just not possible. How can I get her to understand?'

'I fear I do not know the answer to a question which has defeated men for millennia. Perhaps we could move to somewhere we can have a chat?'

They went into the sitting room. Through the open window, the shutters of which had been swung back, a shaft of sunshine brought physical, but no emotional, warmth to the room.

'What more can I possibly tell you? I don't know any more than I've said. I tried to make you understand . . .'

'I need to persuade my superior that while you had a pretty wild argument with Señor Sterne, you did not have any part in his death.'

'He . . . he can't think it was me.'

'He is capable of thinking the most unlikely possibilities. The argument in Ca'n Mortex was in the hall . . .'

Parry interrupted, speaking so quickly, the words tumbled into each other. 'I swear I never attacked him.'

'When you left, you had even more reason to dislike him because of his contemptuous, insulting behaviour, but I am prepared to believe you did not threaten or attack him. Let's talk about that Monday on which he died. Can you remember where and what you did that morning?'

'You think I did kill him or you wouldn't ask.'

'I am trying to prove you did not kill him. Were you here all morning?'

'What day?'

'Monday,' Alvarez repeated.

'We often don't go out then because the clothes shop she likes is shut. She spends so much there that . . .'

'Did you remain here that Monday?'

'I'm trying to remember.'

He noticed Parry's sudden alarm. 'You did go out that day,' he said.

'I . . . I can't be certain.'

'I think you can be.'

'No.'

'Where did you go? Ca'n Mortex?'

'The port. And it wasn't because of what you're thinking,' Parry spoke wildly.

'Then why did you drive there?'

'She said there was another dress shop she had to see. I knew that wasn't the reason.' He spoke dismally, resignedly. 'She hadn't heard from him in days. She was worried he'd dropped her as he had so many others. When we got to the port, she wanted to go for a walk. She tried to sound surprised, not cheered up, when she saw his yacht tied up in the marina. She said we must eat at the yacht club because she was hungry. One of the waiters greeted her, making it obvious she'd been there many times with that tom-cat sod.' Parry seemed about to cry.

'I need your wife to confirm what you have just said. Perhaps you'd ask her to come in here.'

'You . . . you won't say . . . You won't mention what I called him?'

'I'll remain neutral.'

Parry left. It was ten minutes before he returned with Mónika. At first uncooperative, she finally calmed down, agreed she had wanted to visit the dress shop, but had changed her mind; they had had a meal at the yacht club because she had been told they served delicious food.

Alvarez waited, eyelids heavy after the drive to Palma and a siesta which Dolores had insisted on shortening because had it continued much longer, it would have been time to go to bed.

'Yes?' Salas said.

'Inspector Alvarez, señor. I have been to Palma in order to question Señor Parry a second time.'

'A journey which should have been unnecessary.'

'As I said . . .'

'Unnecessary, had you conducted a valid questioning on the first occasion. Have you learned anything?'

'Señor Parry and his wife went to the port that morning and had lunch at the yacht club.'

'And?'

'That's all.'

'You have not obtained independent confirmation he was telling the truth?'

'His wife agreed with what he said.'

'You suggest that is confirmation, when every wife will support her husband even at the cost of lying?'

'That's not always the case.'

'I am glad that I lack your experience.'

'Mónika, given the chance, would have refuted his evidence.'

'Your reason for so extraordinary a statement?'

'She holds him in contempt.'

'Your substitute for logic defeats me.'

'She was having an affair with Señor Sterne.'

'Something you inform me on every possible occasion.'

'She thought Señor Sterne was really taken with her.'

'Taken where?'

'In love with her.'

'You find it necessary to speak gibberish?'

'Since she was in love with him and his wealth, she would never have had any part in his murder. Had she suspected her husband, she would have rushed to report her suspicions. Señor, Parry is mentally and physically incapable of having had any part in the señor's death. He couldn't hurt a fly.'

'Why do you find it necessary to introduce mice, cats, elephants and now flies?'

'It was you who mentioned wild elephants in Andalucia.'

The line was dead.

Alvarez stood by his car in front of Ca'n Mortex and stared out at the bay. Because of the breeze, a large number of yachts and windsurfers were on the water and their sails created a moving image of colour.

'Good evening.'

He turned, faced Roldan.

'I am afraid the señor and señorita are not here, Inspector.'

'Then I'll have a quick word with you.'

'Please come in. Marta is making coffee, so perhaps you'll join us?'

He followed Roldan into the kitchen, greeted Marta, said he would very much like the offered croissant with coffee, sat at the table.

'How's Susanna?' he asked. He noticed the quick glance

they gave each other, hastened to quell any thoughts they might, as parents, have. 'I hope she is better?'

Marta answered. 'She continues to be troubled by a virus.'

'That's bad luck. Viruses can be so debilitating. I expect she's told you I've met her once or twice and had a chat.'

'She said you had been kind.'

'I tried to cheer her up, but didn't succeed. Is there boyfriend problems as well as a virus?'

'At her age, there always is. I tell her, one boy is much like another and there's plenty to go around, but she won't listen.'

The croissant was delicious. Offered a second one with another cup of coffee, he hastened to accept. He had, he admitted, misjudged the Roldans. Marta had seemed starchy and Roldan had had an air of subservience, foreign to a Spaniard, even more so to a Mallorquin. But they were adversely affected by their daughter's ill health, the señor's death, and were, naturally, made uneasy by his continued presence. Few led lives entirely free of peccadilloes and these were often sharply recalled when speaking to a detective.

Roldan offered Alvarez a cigarette, lit a match for them both. 'I may be able to help you, Inspector.'

'Then don't wait.'

'We've had a visitor – the lady we'd only known as Cecilia.'

'Remind me who she is.'

'She phoned here on the day the señor died to ask why he hadn't turned up at the restaurant.'

'Yes, of course.'

'She asked if I knew what was happening about the devil painting.'

'What's that?'

'Perhaps you have not noticed it in the library?'

Alvarez recalled the room. 'There are framed prints of people risking their lives on horses and some paintings, one of them done by a cross-eyed child.'

'That is titled The Devil's Alter Ego.'

'It is well named,' Marta said. 'I think the artist is evil. The picture makes me shiver inside when I look at it.'

'Difficult to know why the señor had such rubbish hanging up.'

'It may look like junk,' Roldan said, 'but it's worth a small fortune.'

'In céntimos?'

'In tens of thousands of euros, the señor once said. An expert was here a couple of months ago. He was writing a book about the painter and his works and I heard him say to the señor, The Devil's Alter Ego was a work of genius.'

'Was he laughing?' Having spoken, Alvarez remembered the insurance list of household goods. A figure of thirty-five thousand euros had been against an unnamed painting by someone or other. Since he had seen nothing to resemble a painting worth even a tenth of that amount, he had dismissed the figure as a mistake by a careless typist. 'Did Cecilia say what her interest in the painting was?'

'The señor had said he would leave it to her and so she wanted to know what was happening. I told her that we knew nothing about it and suggested she spoke to the señor's abogado.'

'Did you learn her name and address?'

'She knew us, of course, but introduced herself as Cecilia Winters in case we had forgotten her. There was no mention of where she lives.'

'Did she come by car or taxi?'

'A private Citröen.'

'Don't suppose you noticed the registration number?'

'In the circumstances I should have done, but . . .'

'I know exactly what you mean. Thanks for telling me about her.'

'Glad to help.'

Seated behind his desk, Alvarez calculated how many years he would have to work in order to make as much as that ugly daub in the library was supposed to be worth. The answer depressed him.

He searched through the telephone directory to try to identify Cecilia Winters. Some Christian names were listed along with surnames, some were not. To save time and his own labour, he assumed, on scant reason, that she lived within easy reach of Llueso. Luck was again with him. C. Winters, Cana Vista.

He checked the time. Too late to intrude on someone's evening, not too late to let the superior chief understand he was still hard at work. He phoned Palma.

'Inspector Alvarez, señor. I should like to inform you I may have learned some important information. I have identified Cecilia.'

'Am I allowed to know who she is and what part she plays in the case?'

'At the time of the señor's death, she phoned Ca'n Mortex to ask why the señor had not turned up at a restaurant. I have spent a long time trying to identify her and have at last succeeded. She is Señora Winters and she lives in Miyorn, near the port. She returned to Ca'n Mortex to ask about the painting she believes will have been left to her in the señor's will.'

'What painting is that?'

'The Devil's Alter Ego which hangs in the library at Ca'n Mortex. In fact, it is not mentioned in the will. It is a very weird painting and it's almost impossible to gain shape or form. The colours are vivid and could have been slapped on . . .'

'Perhaps you will leave your artistic criticism for someone who will appreciate it.'

'I've never heard of the painter.'

'That may be a measure of its quality, but as I have just said . . .'

'Señor, it is insured for thirty-five thousand euros even though most people would throw it into the dustbin. It explains why the señora wanted to know if she was going to get it in return for keeping his bed warm.'

'She was concerned with the running of Señor Sterne's house?'

'No.'

'Then why would she be left something so valuable?'

'"Keeping the bed warm", señor, is a way of describing sexual activity.'

'I should have realized that from the note of interest in your voice. Have you questioned her?'

'I am about . . . I have only just learned her identity and

was on my way to see her when I realized I should inform you before I did so.'

'You did not consider it would have been better to have done so after talking to her so that your report was complete?'

He replaced the receiver. Initiative was ill-rewarded. He lit a cigarette; he poured himself a drink. When there were people foolish enough to pay fortunes for nonsense, a detective's income was derisory. Would he continue to work in the Cuerpo until he was due his pension? How much less would that be than his present pay? He might well have to forgo necessaries, such as a second drink at Club Llueso, another pack of cigarettes, a couple of hundred grammes of the chocolates he so enjoyed . . .

Those who owned and worked the land faced no such deprivations. They weren't thrown out when they attained pensionable age. No, they remained busy and productive, could be optimistic, look to the future for greater success . . .

Years before, Miyorn had been a gentle hill, just beyond Port Llueso, on which grew pine trees, broom, rock roses, rosemary, grass, and the occasional wild orchid. Developers, disliking such natural harmony, had destroyed it. Now, there were houses up and down the hill, flower beds, oleander bushes, even small lawns where terraces had been created.

He stopped at one house at the foot of the hill and asked where Señora Winters lived. The man who answered him was English, had never heard of the person and seemed surprised anyone might think he would. At a second house, a cheerful, middle-aged, plump German lady who spoke good Spanish directed him.

He drove slowly up the tightly turning road, trying not to look to his right; the side of the road was not guarded and although the height was not great, it was quite enough to trigger his altophobia; when he reached Ca Na Vista, he was sweating and his hands were trying to shake.

The house was reasonably named. The mountains around Llueso, Llueso Bay and Playa Neuva were visible, beyond the headlands of the bay, the sea extended to the horizon. To live here was to eat and sleep with the gods; to drive up and down the road was to be watched by expectant Death.

The bungalow was large, with a central frame and two wings. The front door was opened by a woman in her early thirties. Unlikely to be described as beautiful, yet she would quickly attract a man's attention.

'Señora Winters?'

'Yes?'

She had a low, slightly husky voice. She was dressed modestly, but her clothes sharpened her neat figure. He introduced himself. Mention of his rank caused none of the nervous concern he so often met.

'Please come in.'

The sitting room was large, oblong, and the picture window provided a view of Llueso and Llueso Bay. The furniture was of luxury quality. Two small oil paintings on one wall were about as different in style from The Devil's Alter Ego as one could get.

'May I get you a drink, Inspector?'

'Thank you, señora.'

'What would you like?'

'Coñac, with just ice, please.'

She crossed to the near wall, pressed a call button. A woman, older than she, entered and listened to her in silence, left.

'I presume, Inspector, you're here because of poor Keith?'

'That is so, señora. I understand you called at his house after his unfortunate death to ask about a painting.'

'That's right.'

'You wanted to know if he had left it to you in his will. Why did you expect him to have done so?'

'Because he had told me he would.'

'You are married?'

'A sudden change of questioning! I am wearing engagement and wedding rings as you visually checked when we met.'

He had thought his questioning glance had been unobserved. 'Is your husband here?'

'He died three years ago.' She spoke without obvious emotion.

The maid entered, handed a well-filled glass to Alvarez, a flute to Cecilia, left.

'Inspector, why are you interested in the painting?'

'You know The Devil's Alter Ego is by a well-known artist?'

'I've been told that in certain circles, he has a name.'

'It is quite valuable.'

'Seems unlikely.'

'Did Señor Sterne never tell you so?'

'No.'

'I find it rather difficult to believe that.'

'I am sure you suffer many difficulties in your job.'

'It is insured for thirty-five thousand euros.'

'Really!'

He drank and wondered if a cleverer man than he could understand what kind of a woman she was. 'Why did you covet the painting if you did not know its worth?'

'The question of someone who puts value in financial rather than artistic terms.'

'Señora, few would regard it as art.'

'That it is valued highly suggests many do.'

'Because of its lack of shape or form, I cannot imagine many people would wish to own it.'

'Modern art is designed to arouse dislike in the conventional mind.'

'Why do you like it?'

'Why do you like brandy, I, champagne? Who can explain his likes?'

'It has been described as evoking evil.'

'Evil offers many attractions.'

'Will you tell me where you were after noon on Monday, the fifth of the month?'

'That is when Keith died?'

'Yes.'

'You think I murdered him in order to gain possession of the painting? What an imagination you must have!'

'Where were you?'

'I have no idea.'

'It would help you to remember.'

'A threat? You have brought handcuffs? Is there a Black Maria waiting?'

He wished he was sharp enough to counter her mockery. 'You cannot say where you were?'

'You understand perfectly.'

He left. As he drove down the twisting road, not looking to his left, he was annoyed that he had not finished the brandy. It had been a very good one, possibly even a gran reserva Cardenal Mendoza.

FIFTEEN

Alvarez was able to park in front of No. 8. He stepped on to the pavement, used the remote to lock the car, went into the entrada, came to a stop as he recognized Ana's voice. The alternatives. Dull, grey life on a pension, exciting, productive life on many hectares of land.

The inner door opened and Dolores stepped into the entrada. 'Something is keeping you from coming through?'

'I was thinking.'

'It's to be hoped your thoughts don't leave you standing there for the next hour,' she said sharply. 'Ana is here. She was going to leave earlier, but I persuaded her to stay because you'd be so upset if you missed her.'

Would he? If only questions were accompanied by answers.

'You understand what I said?'

He understood that if he were not to annoy her, he must show grateful enthusiasm. 'I'm very glad you managed to persuade her.'

'Then you can come in and say so.'

He followed her into the sitting room.

Ana smiled. 'Hullo, Enrique.'

'What a wonderful surprise.'

'Come and show you're glad to see me.'

He crossed to her chair, leaned over to kiss her cheek. Their lips briefly met.

'I'll pour you a drink,' Jaime said. 'What's it to be? Just the usual double coñac.'

Dolores stood, spoke to Jaime. 'I must get the meal, and you can help me.'

'Do what?'

She ignored the question.

'I'm getting Enrique a drink.'

'He is perfectly capable of doing that for himself.'

Jaime meekly followed her into the kitchen. Alvarez crossed

to the table, poured himself a drink, remembering that in the circumstances it should only be a reasonably sized one.

'I do hope you meant what you said,' Ana paused for confirmation, failed to receive it. 'I had to come into the village to buy one or two things and decided I'd say hullo to Dolores before returning home. She told me I must stay because you'd so hate missing me. Would you?'

He hurried to say: 'Of course.'

'I wonder why?'

She was very presentable; a man could walk with her and not fear silent jeering criticism; for a woman, she was reasonably intelligent. Marry her and retirement from the Cuerpo was to be welcomed, not dreaded.

'You don't know why?' she asked coyly.

He glanced at the bead curtain, knowing Dolores would be listening intently in the kitchen.

'Of course,' she said. 'Very soon, sweet Enrique, you will come to Son Cascall and tell me.'

He escorted Ana to her car. Before getting in, she said: 'Some things must be private, so this is all I can give you now.' She kissed him briefly, settled behind the wheel, drove off.

Dolores was clearing the table. 'So you've finally come to your senses!' She stacked one plate on top of another. 'She has the forgiveness of a saint.'

'I still don't know what she is supposed to be forgiving.'

'A man will lie in his coffin and deny he is dead.'

'Why can't you? . . . Have it your way. I must get a move on. I'm unusually late getting back to work.'

'I doubt any difference will be noted.'

Dolores was proved wrong. Even as he sat behind his desk, the phone rang.

'My secretary,' Salas said, 'has spent the past twenty minutes trying to contact you. No doubt you will tell me you have been engaged.'

'In a sense, I suppose that is so.'

'You like to jest?'

He concentrated on what he was saying. 'Señor, I have been trying to identify other women who were friendly with Señor Sterne.'

'Have you succeeded?'

'Unfortunately, not.'

'Why not?'

'The nature of the problem makes it a very difficult task.'

'Perhaps you are judging it to be beyond your ability? Have you questioned Señora Winters?'

'Yes, señor.'

'With what result?'

'It's difficult to say.'

'Why?'

'I found her to be a very strange woman.'

'She will no doubt have had reason to believe you an unusual inspector.'

'I asked her where her husband was. She replied he was dead.'

'It is not unusual for a husband to die before his wife.'

'Yet, she showed not the slightest emotion.'

'She is English?'

'Yes.'

'They have iced water in their veins.'

'Judging by a book I read, especially when it's blue.'

'What stupidity are you saying now?'

'Cecilia accepts she called at Ca'n Mortex and asked about the painting, The Devil's Alter Ego, which the señor had promised to leave to her. She denies she believed it was worth a fraction of the sum for which it is insured.'

'Then why was she so eager to get her hands on it?'

'I don't know.'

'It would not, of course, have occurred to you that that was a question to be asked.'

'But I did ask, señor. Much of her answer was confusing. When I mentioned someone had described the painting as emanating a sense of evil, she remarked that evil had its attractions.'

'Why should that confuse you? You interest yourself in matters most would term evil.'

'I asked her to name where she had been at the time of the señor's death. She had no idea. When I pointed out it would assist her to give an answer, she seemed to be amused.'

'No doubt because of the naivety of your questioning. It is all too clear that your claim to have made a breakthrough in the case was nonsense.'

'What I said, señor, was I might have done so, not that I had.'

'I am more aware of what you said than you are. To any officer other than you, this incident would show the peril of making bombastic claims that are quickly shown to be without any substance.'

The call was concluded.

The late sunshine made Marcial sweat as he used a mattock to clear the few weeds which had broken surface among the as-yet unwatered carrots. He leaned on the haft as he watched Alvarez approach.

'I've a couple more questions.'

'You've so many, you're like a man what's eaten too many beans.'

'Won't keep you from work for long.'

'But as it'll keep you away from it, as long as you can take.'

Alvarez stared at a row of sweetcorn. 'Looks about ready for picking.'

'Glad you've told me so as I know.'

'Strange to think years back it was thought of as only animal food. Took the foreigners to teach us how good it can be.'

'And how bad other things can be.'

'True. Nothing is ever either just positive or negative.'

'Ever told an electrician that?'

Alvarez used a handkerchief to remove the sweat from his face. 'How about moving out of the sun into the shade?'

'You need life to be nice and comfortable?'

They walked along one of the rough paths, topped with small stones taken from the soil, and sat under the shade of a lemon tree. They smoked, each enjoying the peace and contentment, however brief, a countryman could gain from the setting.

'I want to know about that Monday,' Alvarez said as he stubbed out his cigarette in the soil.

'Told you. But you want to learn if I say something different so as you can start shouting it was me did him in?'

'How were things when you came to work and during the morning?'

'Same as ever.'

'When did you come to work?'

'Eight, like my job says.'

'I'm asking when you arrived, not when you were supposed to.'

'Not met anyone before who likes to earn his pay?'

'I believe they do exist. Was it quiet at the house?'

'Seemed so.'

'What was the first sign of movement?'

'Upstairs shutters were swung back.'

'When did you first see anyone from inside?'

'The brother and sister drove off.'

'Before or after your break for coffee?'

'An hour, hour and a half, like I told you.'

'And then?'

'They came back.'

'According to your belly, that was around midday?'

'Ain't ever far out.'

'Any idea where they'd been?'

'Think they came over for a chat? All they ever do is give orders and tell me I'm doing things wrong.'

'Were there any visitors before the señor was discovered?'

'I told you there was.'

'You mentioned a car which turned into the drive as you were leaving on your mobylette for lunch. You reckon it was a small black Citröen hatchback.'

'What's wrong with that?'

'Nothing. It agrees with what Evaristo has said. You saw the driver?'

'No.'

'Last time, you told me you did.'

'I told you it was being driven too quick, and I was a bloody sight more concerned with not being knocked dead that seeing who was the bloody fool driving.'

'But it was definitely a man?'

'With two heads and four arms.'

'Lighten up.'

'It was a man.'

'And you've no idea who he was?'

'Never studied enough backs of heads to tell one from another.'

'Was there anything noticeable about the car?'

'Only what I said last time.'

'The dangling skeleton?'

'If that's what it was.'

'Where did you eat that day?'

'Had what the wife give me.'

'You didn't get to enjoy Marta's cooking?'

'Maybe had a little of what was going when I got back here.'

'You were there until when?'

'Can't rightly say.'

'Your belly was enjoying a siesta?'

'We was talking more than usual.'

'Translated, that means you were in the kitchen long after you should have resumed work. You weren't worried the señor would find you there?'

'He never went near the kitchen.'

'He might have first looked for you in the garden.'

'Too big for that.'

'Plenty of skiving places?'

'Tell me you don't ever help yourself to a bit of time off and I'll laugh.'

'When d'you reckon you went back to work?'

'Might have been a bit late.'

'Half an hour, an hour?'

'Give over. Ten minutes at the most.'

'You were in the kitchen all that time with Roldan and Marta?'

'Yes.'

'When did you learn Roldan had found the señor, dead in his car?'

'When he shouted.'

'What did you do when you learned what was the trouble?'

'Looked to see.'

'You went down into the garage?'

'No.'

'Didn't occur you might have been able to help him?'

'Someone wants to commit suicide, let him.'

'It wasn't suicide.'

'Wasn't to know that, was I?'

'Are the brother and sister here now?'

'Ain't see 'em leave.'

He stood. 'You're growing more yellow tomatoes. Some must like 'em. What do they taste like?'

'Buy some and find out.'

'Not seen them on sale and I wasn't trying to cadge.'

'Wouldn't have succeeded.'

He walked to the house, went into the kitchen. Marta was cooking. 'Something smells delicious.'

She stirred the contents of the casserole on one of the gas rings on top of the oven. 'Maybe them inside will think it tastes good and stop complaining.'

'They can't have much to complain about.'

'You reckon that stops them?'

'You've said they got on quite well with the señor.'

'They weren't going to upset him and get kicked out of all their free living.'

'He might have done that if they'd annoyed him?'

'There wasn't much knowing what he was likely to do, except bring in another woman as soon as one left.'

'Did his women bother you?'

'When the señor pays the salary, you don't let yourself be bothered.'

But from her manner, there had been times when she had found it difficult to conceal her feelings. 'I need to talk to the brother and sister. Are they here?'

'As far as I know. But they don't tell me anything, so they could have left hours ago.'

'I'll see if I can find them.'

'If you ask me, I wouldn't go looking very hard.'

He smiled. 'By the way, I met Cecilia. She'd no idea that painting was valuable.'

'Easy to say.'

'She just enjoyed it as a painting.'

'Must be a strange life she leads.'

He chatted a while longer, left the kitchen and went through to the hall. From the green sitting-room came the sound of speech and from the evenness of the rhythm, he judged it was from the television. He opened the door, stepped inside.

They stared at him with surprise. Caroline was the first to speak.

· 'How dare you come in here.'

'Señorita, in the hall, I tried to attract your attention, but failed. I had to enter unannounced.'

'You think you can do as you damn well like?'

'Far from it. But I do have to do anything which might help to uncover the circumstances of your father's death.'

'That means breaking into the house and forcing your way into this room?'

'I have explained, señorita. If you will now just tell me . . .'

'I've told you all I know.'

'I think, perhaps not.'

'You're insolently suggesting I or my brother is withholding evidence?'

'Not yet knowing all the circumstances, I regretfully have to consider the possibility.'

'My God! How you police lack any intelligence.'

'That may seem to you to be so, señorita; for our part, we have to learn how to deal with the stupidity of tourists.'

'You'll regret saying that.'

'One seldom regrets a pleasure. Tell me about the Monday morning on which your father unfortunately died.'

'If you think I'm going to sit here and hear you trying to imply I murdered him, you're a bigger fool than you appear.'

Alec Sterne, voice pitched high, said: 'For Pete's sake, calm it, sis.'

'You expect me to sit back and let him insult me?'

'You did insult him first.'

Alvarez was surprised Alec Sterne should challenge her. Perhaps he did possess the shadow of a character. 'Señora, is it correct that on the Monday, you and your brother drove away from here in the morning?'

'Yes.'

'At what time did you leave?'

'I've no idea.'

'Would you like to estimate a time?'

'No.'

'Why not?'

Alec Sterne said hastily: 'It was a little after nine.'

'Thank you, señor. And when did you return?'

'About midday.'

'You cannot be more precise?'

'I'm afraid not.'

'Did you stay here for long?'

'No.'

'Why did you return?'

'I can't remember.'

'Are you certain?'

'I'd tell you if I could. Maybe one of us had forgotten something.'

'You can suggest what?'

'No. It must have been unimportant.'

'Yet important enough to force your return?' Alvarez waited for a reply, finally said: 'Did you speak to the señor during the time you were here?'

'We didn't see him.'

'I know what you're thinking,' she said shrilly. 'You're so damned prejudiced, you're determined to believe we had something to do with father's death.'

'Señorita, it is not prejudice which makes me ask questions, it is the fact that you seem both to have been in this house when your father died.'

'You can't know that for sure. And even if we were, that doesn't mean we killed him.'

'You might have threatened him, caused him such shocked fear, he died.'

'Are you deaf as well as dumb? Didn't you hear my brother say we didn't see or speak to him? Are you incapable of understanding what that means?'

'Not incapable, but I need to know whether you are both lying.'

'You bastard,' she shouted.

Alec Sterne said, with nervous haste: 'Inspector, she's very upset over father's death and shocked you could believe either of us guilty of parricide.'

'As one would imagine. So perhaps you would explain to her that the best way of avoiding so unwelcome a possibility is to help me with my enquiries.'

There was a silence.

'Señorita, you did not know where your father was when you were briefly back in the house?'

'I keep telling you so.' She spoke more calmly.

'You were not surprised you did not meet him?'

'We didn't rush to speak to him every time we returned.'

'Your relationship with him was strained?'

'We're not like you lot.'

Alec Sterne said: 'We're not so openly sentimental, Inspector.'

'I understand that. Señorita, why did you return to the house and then leave so quickly afterwards?'

'It doesn't matter.'

'Do I need to explain it might have been that after the initial shock of what had happened, one of you thought to conceal the truth by imitating suicide?'

'I had to come back for a reason that's none of your goddamn business.'

'You remember that after his death, your father lay on the floor of the garage before his body was picked up and placed in his car?'

'You hate us, don't you?'

'No, señorita.'

'You can't stand seeing the difference between you and someone with breeding and manners. I came back . . . because I am a woman. Can you understand now or do I have to explain it in full to give you the pleasure of embarrassing me further?'

'I gain no pleasure from distressing anyone.' He spoke to Alec Sterne. 'Have you been in touch with the company which issued your father's assurance policy?'

'Should I have done?'

'It would be advisable. Remember, you will need a certificate of death and of identification to accompany your actual claim . . . Do you remember my asking if a car approached here as you drove out on the last occasion?'

'We never noticed one.'

'A black hatchback did not approach the gates and signal it was turning in as you drove away?'

'With all the traffic on the road in the summer, it's impossible to be certain what other cars are going to do. Does it matter we didn't see it?'

'There was just the off-chance you might have noticed it. I need disturb you no longer. Thank you both for your help.'

'Not given voluntarily,' she said bitterly.

SIXTEEN

A sharp 'Yes, what is it?' startled Alvarez, having waited to speak to Salas.

'Inspector Alvarez reporting, señor. I have many, many further enquiries concerning Señor Sterne's death. I have questioned Marcial, the gardener at Ca'n Mortex, also Señor and Señorita Sterne, the son and daughter.'

'You surprise me.'

'For what reason, señor?'

'I might have been listening to a report from an efficient officer.'

'I have learned nothing new. However, the evidence of each has remained consistent, even to the dangling skeleton.'

'You understand what you are saying?'

'It's referring to one of those dangling things at the end of a cord which some people hang up behind the back windows of their cars. They must have very juvenile minds.'

'I have one in my car.'

'What I meant was . . .'

'My wife is very fond of corgis. She saw one of "those dangling things", as you ignorantly called it, which featured a corgi.'

'That's very different, señor.'

'Different from what?'

'A skeleton.'

'I understood you were objecting to the concept, not the specifics.'

'No, señor. I must have misjudged my words.'

'A common failing. Perhaps you will now move on and deal with matters of importance, not ones of no account.'

'The skeleton is of some importance, señor.'

'In what way?'

'Marcial's evidence supports Roldan's. Further, whilst many people like to have dangling things in their cars, especially when there is an emotional reason to do so, not many would choose a skeleton because it might be inviting death to have the last laugh. Therefore, if a car is observed that is a black hatchback, almost certainly a Citröen, which sports a skeleton, then there is good reason to identify that as the one the staff saw. Naturally, one has to be prepared for a coincidence, but I would think the combination of known details would make this unusual . . .'

'Can they describe the driver?'

'As I reported before, señor, neither of them gained more than a view of the back of his head. Roldan because he was looking from behind the car, Marcial because he was in a tangle with his mobylette.'

'How do you intend identifying the driver?'

'Apart from having the fortune of seeing him in the car, it seems to me we must hope for the luck . . .'

'I am confident that you are the first inspector in the history of the Cuerpo who has admitted that his inability to pursue an investigation with efficiency means he has to rely on luck to reach any conclusion.'

'But in the circumstances . . .'

'I need to tell you what to do. You will draw up a list of possible cars and question the owners.'

'But . . . Señor, all we know for certain is that the car was probably a Citröen, black and a hatchback. To list all the cars with those features . . . It's a task that would defeat Homer.'

'I assume, in a hopeless attempt to appear literate, you mean Hercules.'

'I just can't see . . .'

'Wilful blindness follows an acceptance of failure. Is it not reasonable to assume the driver was friendly with Sterne.'

'I doubt that he was.'

'Why?'

'I don't think Sterne, with his lifestyle, would be friendly with someone who hung a . . . With someone who did not drive a much larger and more expensive car.'

'It is probable that the driver wished to speak to Sterne.'

'Then why didn't he make himself known to the staff?'

'As I have cause to know well, it is not every member of

one's staff who attends to his duties. The visitor may have rung the bell or knocked and not been heard because the staff were too busy loitering at the back of the house. He may suddenly have changed his mind, or remembered something he needed to do before speaking to someone.'

'Or, never having met the señor, perhaps he was going to Ca'n Mortex to ask for a contribution to a fund to help someone in trouble and knowing the señor was wealthy, hoped he would give generously.'

'It is difficult to conceive a more unlikely possibility.'

'I don't think that's any more far-fetched than your suggestions.'

'Such lack of judgement is to be expected. As a friend, or at least an acquaintance, of the señor, he will be known to the staff. They can provide names and addresses. You will question them to determine which of them was the driver of this car.'

'The staff were never introduced to guests.'

'You imagine they would be?'

'Then how do they know who any of them were?'

'You lack experience in many things, including domestic staff. Such people display great initiative in learning matters which do not concern them. You will question them as I have ordered. You have questioned Señorita Sterne again?'

'Yes, señor.'

'Is it naive to hope that you behaved with far more respect than before?'

'She is a difficult person.'

'For the explanation of her difficulty, one needs to look to the questioner.'

'You did say that you found her impossibly rude.'

'I may have said she was a little difficult, that is all. Was she able to provide any fresh evidence?'

'She was very reluctant even to speak to me. Was outraged that I seemed to think that she or her brother might have had a part in their father's death.'

'Having been unable to make any progress in the case, you accused her of her father's murder?'

'She was being so uncooperative, I asked her if she had

reason to fear my questioning – this caused her to complain I was accusing her and her brother. She would not estimate the time when they left the house on Monday morning.

'I asked Señor Alec Sterne if he had been in touch with the company which had insured his father's life and he said he had not. That may be a significant omission.'

'Why?'

'If he killed his father to gain from the insurance policy, it is probable he would have been in touch with the company immediately.'

'You have reason for claiming that?'

'Years ago, I was involved in a similar case, on a very much smaller scale, and the murderer was in touch with the company within hours. A criminal is eager to gain the rewards of his crime, but I think it's just as likely the haste is to prove to himself that the gain justified the means.'

'Any acceptance of such a possibility needs the originator to be someone far better qualified to make it.'

'It has to mean something that Alec Sterne has not begun to make a claim.'

'It is to be hoped you manage to uncover evidence of a far more significant nature when you can bring yourself to carry out your orders.'

Alvarez, knowing the reception he was likely to receive, phoned Trafico. 'I'm looking for a car.'

'Hope you manage to find one.'

'A black Citröen hatchback.'

'There are plenty of 'em around so you should manage to fix a bit of a discount.'

Those who worked in traffic were known to be facetious as a way of relieving the boredom of their task. 'It's a murder case.'

There was a change in attitude. 'What's the registration number?'

'Not known.'

'Colour?'

'Black.'

'Owner's name?'

'Can't say. But it's likely he lives near Llueso.'

'Am I wrong to think you are asking us to trace a car about which all you know is that it's a black hatchback Citröen?'

'Yes.'

'You are a comedian?'

'If you draw up a list of all possible cars with their owners' names and addresses . . .'

'I'd need my head examined.'

'The superior chief wants the list.'

'Then he also needs a psychiatrist.'

'Do I tell him you refuse to draw it up?'

The line was dead. Alvarez replaced the receiver. He supposed that had he been approached with a request of such an insubstantial nature he would have responded in similar form.

He lit a cigarette.

There were times when the fog of life was not just poet-talk. Occasionally, murder was motiveless – a random killing, mistaken identity – but had that been the case, the murderer would not have put the body in the car to simulate suicide. So there had been motive. Yet those who had been identified as having motives were able to establish their innocence. There was the probability of a cuckolded husband seeking his revenge, but how to identify him? The driver of the black Citröen must come under sharp suspicion, even when his motive was unknown, but only Salas thought he could be identified.

If only the medical and forensic evidence had shown Sterne to have died from monoxide poisoning, had not lain on the floor of the garage before being found seated in the car, it would have been suicide and he would not be trying to unravel a Gordian knot.

He poured himself a drink. Sterne had died from severe fright. Someone had caused him to suffer that extreme emotion. That someone was legally a murderer, even if he had had no reason to suspect his anger might kill. Who had reason for such hatred?

He poured himself a second drink. He must return to the beginning. Question those he had already questioned and suffer

Caroline's bitching; cross-check facts; speak to female expatri-
ates and hope to learn which of them had been over-friendly
with Sterne . . .

Caroline. Hard steel while her brother was weak tin. He
had accepted her reason for returning to the house, embarrassed
at doubting her answer. A woman as sharp as she would guess
that would be his reaction, so how better to prevent his
questioning her further? She and her brother had probably
been in the house when their father died. They claimed they
had not expected to speak to him, had not even seen him
during the time they were in Ca'n Mortex. It was a large house
and they had no love for their father, so it was feasible they
would not have sought him to have a word. Half a million
pounds provided a strong motive. Alec Sterne denied he had
been in touch with the assurance company which had provided
some reason to consider their possible innocence. Had he been
telling the truth?

There were those who would dismiss potatoes as peasants'
food. Not when Patatas a la Riojana was cooked by Dolores
– potatoes, chorizo, tomatoes, pimientos, onions, stock,
seasoning, olive oil. César Ritz would have been pleased to
present the dish.

'Is there some more?' Jaime asked.

'I think the children finished it before they went out to play,'
Dolores answered.

'They never think of others.'

'Have you given them cause to do so?'

'A working man needs to eat his fill.'

'When he works.'

'Are you saying I don't?'

'A question which does not call for an answer.'

'Who keeps the house going?'

'I'll go on holiday and you will learn. Right now, you can
help me clear the table.'

'Again?'

She stood. 'I'll take the dishes, you bring the rest.'

When once more seated at the table, Dolores cracked a
walnut. 'You are seeing Ana this evening, Enrique?'

'I don't know.'

'Why not?'

'It depends if I can get away from work in good time.'

'You can. Do you have the ring ready?'

'What ring?'

'Have you spent all morning visiting bars? The engagement ring, of course.'

'Why do I need one?'

'Aiyee! But as my dear mother so often had reason to say, the Lord God took Adam's brain as well as his rib to create woman.'

'I haven't said anything definite to her.'

'She has to you,' Jaime remarked.

Dolores, her tone noticeably sharper, said: 'You will have to tell her you couldn't see any ring she might like at the local jewellers, so you'll take her into Palma.'

'That'll cost him a fortune,' Jamie said.

'You are empty of sentiment?'

'Sentiment doesn't put euros into the pocket.'

'Enrique,' she said, 'you should take her yellow and red roses when you tell her about Palma.'

'They must grow enough flowers . . .'

'Have you never learned how to behave towards a lady? Casa Danera usually has very nice roses.'

'For which they charge very nice prices,' Jaime said.

'At such a moment, you think Enrique's only interest is money?'

'Why else would . . .' He stopped abruptly as Dolores glared at him.

She ate a walnut, reached across for another one. 'Of course, you will need a new suit; the only one you have looks as if you found it in a rubbish skip. I will find out who is the best tailor. And where do you think the marriage luncheon should be held? Casa Tramuntana is probably the best.'

'And the most expensive.'

She ignored her husband's comment. 'Where will you go for the honeymoon?'

'If I do decide to . . . We'd be getting on a bit for that sort of thing.'

'You have no thought for Ana? You would return her to Son Cascall as if it were just another day?'

'It seems unnecessary to bother about all that sort of thing, especially when she's been married before.'

'Only you could speak with so little heart. I was talking to Ana. Ever since she was a child, she has wanted to visit Argentina. You can take her there for your honeymoon.'

'Lucky for him she doesn't want to go to Australia,' Jaime said.

She cracked the walnut with unnecessary force.

As Alvarez walked to his parked car, carrying a large bunch of roses wrapped in tissue paper, secured with red ribbon, he hoped no one from the post would see him. A cabo's amusement would be shared with all.

He reached his car, unobserved as far as he could judge, settled behind the wheel. His mind drifted back in time. He was in a paseo, hurrying or loitering in the outer circle in order to murmur sweet words to Rosalie as they briefly came abreast of each other; declaring his love to Carmen, suffering the humiliation of her sneering remark that she would not consider marrying a peasant; the hours he had spent by the hospital bedside of Juana María, silently, hopelessly hoping she would live.

He drove slowly, his thoughts returned to the present. What, he asked himself for the umpteenth time, if he had been misled? Having had reason to dismiss her husband, naturally Ana was lonely and welcomed contact with others. She liked him because they had a common interest – land, farming, the satisfaction of eating an orange just plucked from the tree . . .

He turned into the earth and stone drive. Son Cascall, backed by the mountains with their crests still in sunshine, was the epitome of strength and durability, the crops, proof of the land's fecundity.

Ana opened the front door. He handed her the roses.

'I knew you had to be one of the few men with the heart to know what yellow and red roses mean,' she said, before she kissed him.

SEVENTEEN

The garden in front of Ca'n Mortex was a carpet of colour. If each flower was worth a quarter of what he had been charged for each rose, Alvarez wondered how many euros he was looking at.

Roldan opened the door. 'Good morning, Inspector.'

'Do you have radar to tell you when someone's coming here?'

He smiled. 'I happened to be in the front sitting-room when you drove in.'

'Are they here?'

'The señor and señorita left soon after breakfast.'

'Have you any idea when they'll be back?'

'They have asked Marta to have a meal ready at one. The English eat early.'

'Filetes con foie-gras?'

'I don't know what she's cooking, but I doubt it will be that. They don't seem to care what they eat and never say they've enjoyed a meal.'

'That must annoy her.'

'She still cooks as if they were gourmets. When we're certain what's happening here, we'll quit domestic work. How does one know what an employer is like until one has started to work for him? There may be many employers like those two. We'll start a restaurant and know people go there because they like and appreciate the food. We've saved a bit and it's long been an idea of ours.'

'I've been told it's very hard work.'

'We've never minded that.'

Strange, Alvarez thought.

'Come on through.'

In the kitchen, Roldan spoke to his wife. 'The inspector wants to see the señor and señorita. I told him they've gone out, but should be back for lunch. He might like some coffee before he decides what to do.'

'I'll make some right away. And there are the croissants they didn't want at breakfast. Go with the inspector into the staff room and I'll bring them in.'

'What's wrong with staying here?' Alvarez asked.

'You don't mind the kitchen?'

'The most important room in the house.'

He and Roldan sat at the table. She loaded the coffee machine, placed three plates on the table, on one of which were two croissants. 'Please help yourself. And do you like a drop of coñac to enliven the coffee?'

'Several drops to get it singing,' Roldan said.

'You'll find it in the usual place.'

The coffee was generously 'enlivened', the croissants – he had been pressed to have both – were almost as delicious as when they had been bought newly baked. He had just been given a second cup of coffee when Susanna, wearing a nightdress, hurried into the kitchen.

'Mum, I've just been . . .' She stopped as she saw Alvarez.

He greeted her. She murmured something.

'Come on, love.' Marta hurried over to her daughter. 'Let's get you back to bed.' She supported Susanna as they left.

'They've still not been able to get rid of the virus?' Alvarez asked.

'They keep changing treatments, but nothing works.'

'It must be very worrying for you and your wife.'

'It's bloody hell.'

'I had to learn some years ago how one never suffers greater mental pain than when watching someone else in physical pain. Is there anything I can do to help?'

'No one can do anything.'

'There's a specialist at Son Dureta who will always help the police. If I ask him for the name of the top man in viruses in Spain . . .'

Roldan said violently: 'Can't you understand? Nothing can be done.' He drank the remaining coffee in his cup. 'I'm sorry.'

'For what?'

'Shouting at you when you were trying to help.'

Marta returned, sat. 'She's lying down again.'

Alvarez wished there were words which could help, judged none could. Personal grief could be impregnable.

'Have you told the inspector?' she asked.

'I was going to when Susanna . . .'

She cut short her husband's words. 'I saw that car again when I was in the village.'

'It probably wasn't the same one,' Roldan said.

'I'm certain it was. And it's no good you saying anything when you weren't there.'

'When and where did you see it?' Alvarez asked.

'I was shopping this morning; approaching the new square, the traffic had come to a stop. I looked at the cars, wondering what the problem was, and noticed a black one which had a dancing skeleton inside the window. I'm certain it was the same car.'

'Did you know what make it was?'

'A Citröen.'

'Who was in it?'

'Just the driver.'

'Did you see his face?'

'Only when he looked sideways and waved at a passer-by.'

'Can you describe him?'

'Not really.'

'What was the shape of his head? Oval, carroty, round?'

'Seemed to be round.'

'Was his hair black, brown, or grey? Was it straight, curly, or was he balding; had he shaved his head?'

'It was just an ordinary brown and straight.'

'Were his ears a funny shape?'

'I wouldn't have said they were any different to normal.'

'Beard or clean shaven?'

'Like what they call designer stubble.'

'Were his lips thick, thin?'

'Can't really say.'

'What was he wearing?'

'All I could see was a kind of T-shirt. Light blue.'

'Is there anything more you can remember?'

'As it drew away, I remembered to have a look at the registration number. But then another car got in the way.'

'You weren't able to read it?'

'Only the letters.'

'What were they?'

'C I M. They're my sister's initials. Carolina Inés Margarita.'

'You've been a great help,' he assured her.

Caroline and Alec Sterne had not returned by twenty past one.

'And it's supposed to be us who can't keep time.' Marta walked over to the stove and turned down the temperature of the oven.

'I'd better forget them and return home or I'll miss out on lunch.' Alvarez stood.

'Why not stay and eat here? Even if them two don't care what they're having, you look like you do. Marcial is returning home for his meal because his wife's none too well and he won't be wanting any – always offer him some of what we're eating. I'm proud of my Terena Rellena, so maybe you'd like to try it?'

'I most certainly would.' Veal stuffed with bacon, ham, olives, eggs, onion, shallot, mushrooms, and seasoning.

He phoned Dolores and apologized for his coming absence.

'You are dining with Ana?'

Dolores would be annoyed if he did not offer a good reason – one she considered good – for not returning home. Ana would have provided that, but she and Ana were on close terms and it was almost certain she would learn his excuse had been a lie. 'The superior chief has told me to work through.'

'And will he also forgo lunch?'

'I doubt it. If there's the chance, I'll buy a couple of sandwiches at the petrol station.'

'I'll make certain you have a good supper.'

It seemed he was going to enjoy a delicious lunch and a delicious supper. It was known as gain-gain.

Marcial was back at work at the far end of the kitchen garden. Alvarez crossed to where he was irrigating three rows of tomatoes, there being no standing pipes.

'How's the wife?' he asked.

'What's it to you?'

'They said inside that she wasn't well.'

'Just a touch of fever.'

'Sorry to hear that.'

Marcial used a mattock to open one of the channels by scooping out a plug of earth and then used this to dam the channel which had just been running.

'I've not seen them cultivated like that before,' Alvarez said, as he pointed at the nearest tomatoes, each supported by a thin bamboo cane.

'You saw 'em the other day.'

'Are these red ones as good as the yellow ones?'

'Prefer 'em to be red; seems more natural. But they both taste.'

'I wouldn't mind trying one.'

'Then best start growing 'em.'

'With the señor dead, what do you do with everything?'

'Same as always; take most to the house, keep some for home. And if you're thinking evil, like you blokes do, the señor said as I could.'

'I wouldn't doubt it.'

'You'd doubt yourself.'

'Did you see a black car drive away from the house on the day the señor died?'

'Ain't I said?'

'You reckon it was a Citröen hatchback.'

'You remember?'

'You described yourself as shocked when it near knocked you for six.'

'You get knocked flying by a car and learn how you feel.'

'You could have been too shocked to notice anything accurately. Can you remember what colour it was?'

'Black.'

'A saloon?'

'Hatchback. Shall I write it all down so as you can remember what you've been telling?'

'What else did you notice about the car?'

'It had four wheels.'

'That'll help to identify it. Anything else?'

'You think I made a close inspection?'

'I think you must have been more dazed than you reckon. There wasn't something conspicuous about it?'

'Are you talking about that bloody stupid thing?'

'I can't be certain until you identify it.'

'Dangling on a bit of a string?'

'What was?'

'If you got paid for asking daft questions, you'd be rich.'

'If I got paid for listening to stupid answers, I'd be richer.'

Marcial used the mattock to open another channel, dam the one which had been running.

'You can't say what it was?'

'Likely a skeleton.'

'What about the registration number?'

'Like I said before . . .'

'Maybe you can remember better now.'

'And perhaps I can't.'

'What colour hair did the driver have?'

'Don't know and don't give a bugger.'

After a soothing brandy, Alvarez phoned Salas.

'Yes?'

'I have just been speaking to . . .'

'You are?'

'Señor, recently when we spoke, you said it was a waste of time to give my name as your secretary had done so.'

'That is an excuse for your present failure?'

'It seems logical that . . .'

'Logic is a word that sits too lightly on your tongue. Do you intend to name yourself?'

'Inspector Alvarez.'

'It should not need me to determine whom I am addressing. Where are you?'

'Llueso.'

'Why are you phoning?'

'To make a report.'

'Then make it and waste no more of my time.'

Alvarez did so.

'You are satisfied that the car seen by the woman was the same as earlier seen by the two men on the day the señor died?'

'There is the possibility it could be.'

'You accept the possibility is slight?'

'Naturally, señor. However, the dancing skeleton added to type and colour of car must provide a reasonably solid identification. One seldom sees skeletons on dangles in cars. Dogs are far more common and appropriate. I once saw an extraordinary . . .'

'I am uninterested in what will undoubtedly be a prurient memory. Being able to provide the three letters will enable Trafico to provide a shorter list, more quickly.'

'Especially when they restrict the area in which the owner is living.'

'You have learned he lives locally?'

'No, but it seems likely.'

'On what grounds?'

'As I have mentioned before, he must have known Señor Sterne.'

'That precludes his living in Palma. Or even in England?'

'No. But if I am to make more progress, I have to work with probabilities, not just certainties.'

'Have you made any progress?'

'For the moment, unfortunately not as much as I would hope.'

'You find no discredit in admitting that?'

'I have questioned a great number of people and determined they could not be guilty. I have . . .'

'What you have not done is to understand there is no reason to believe this was a motiveless murder and therefore motive is the key to its solution.'

'I made that point from the beginning, señor.'

'Had you done so, I should not have to remark on your failure.'

'I've uncovered several possible motives and followed them up, without success, as you know.'

'I am only too aware of that.'

'The only motive I can now suggest – apart from an enraged husband – is the five hundred thousand pounds from the life assurance. The fact that Alec Sterne has made no attempt to inform the company of his father's death . . .'

'How do you know that?'

'He told me so.'

'You have spoken to the company and asked them to confirm they have not been informed of Señor Sterne's death?'

Due to the pressure of work and domestic problems, he had forgotten to phone. 'Señor, the company were unable to answer me immediately and said they would ring back when they had the answer.'

'How long ago was that?'

'I suppose it was a day or two.'

'You have not spoken to them again to find out why you haven't heard from them?'

'I intend to do so after speaking to you.'

'Have you questioned the brother and sister to establish whether they have valid alibis, or is that something more you may do after speaking to me?'

'As I think I have told you . . .'

'You will answer the question directly and not try to evade it.'

'I have done so more than once. Their evidence has not altered. They drove out from Ca'n Mortex at about nine in the morning. They returned at around twelve because the señorita wished to return home. They agree they were in the house at the time of their father's death, but claim they did not speak to him or see him before they left. They saw no reason for that to cause any surprise.'

'In your own words, they remain the persons known to have a motive, who can offer no alibis, yet you have been unable to obtain any information which would indicate, let alone prove, their guilt. You have obviously failed to question them pugnaciously.'

'You will remember, señor, she is not a person who it is easy to question pugnaciously.'

'You will not take it upon yourself to tell me what I remember. Question them again and this time impose such personality as you possess and make it very obvious you will uncover the truth.'

'Perhaps . . .'

'Recently, you have constantly introduced animals into your weak analogies and that is to be deplored. However, since this childish habit seems to be the only way in which you can

appreciate human relationships, you will think of yourself as
a cat and the woman as a mouse.'

'I play with her, señor?'

The line was dead. Alvarez poured himself another brandy,
searched for the notes he had made, eventually found them in
one of the drawers of the desk. He read through them to remind
himself of the name of the assurance company. He asked
Telefonica to determine the number of the Diamond Assurance
Company in Birmingham. True to form, the operator objected
to the task on the grounds of impossibility before finally
accepting she might be able to do as asked.

He phoned the company. A woman asked him whom he
wanted; when he answered, he was told to press 7. He pressed
7, was eventually told to press 9. He listened to five minutes
of The Four Seasons before he was told to press 2. To his
relief, he had reached the end of the treasure trail.

'You're asking if Mr Alec Sterne has advised us of the death
of his father, Keith Sterne?'

'That's right.'

'I'll have to be given the authority to answer you. You are
Inspector Alvarez, of the Cuerpo General de Policia in
Mallorca.'

'Yes.'

'What's the weather like your way?'

'Very hot and sunny.'

'Here, it's raining like the Second Flood. Hang on and I'll
have a word with Mr James.'

Alvarez listened to more, or was it a repeat, of The Four
Seasons.

'Hullo, sorry for the delay. I've checked and can tell you
Alec Sterne phoned on the fifth of July and informed us of
his father's death and asked for confirmation of the policy.'

'Did he want to know when payment of the assured sum
would be made?'

'Yes. He was told he must provide us with a death certificate, a confirmation of identity from the consul, and certain
legal requirements must be met before that could be done.'

Alvarez thanked the other. He leaned back in his chair. He
would question Alec Sterne the next day and now had the

ammunition to do so 'pugnaciously'. He checked the time.
Salas was unlikely to phone until well after lunch, so there
was no reason against his leaving the office and having a
drink at Club Llueso before returning home for a drink and
lunch.

Jaime was seated at the dining-room table on which was a
bottle and a half-filled glass. He waited until Alvarez sat before
he said excitedly: 'You'll never guess who I met earlier.'

'Then there's no point in trying.' Alvarez brought a glass
out of the sideboard and poured himself a brandy, added three
cubes of ice.

'Enrique,' came the call from the kitchen, 'have you spoken
to Ana?'

'Not today.'

'Why not?'

'I've been at work.'

Her head came through the bead curtain. 'You think that a
good reason?'

'I can't do two things at once.'

'That you should believe your work was more important
than speaking to her! Romance is a word that is foreign to
you. You must phone her now.'

'Why?'

'Sweet Mary! Do you need to be taught that to eat you must
open your mouth? You phone to tell her it has been an empty
day for you since you have not seen her.'

'Talk like that and she'll think he's been reading women's
tosh,' Jaime said.

'What is "women's tosh"?'

'Books which are all lovey-dovey; she looks into his eyes
and feels ants crawling up her spine.'

She withdrew her head and seconds later banged a saucepan
against the cooker to express her annoyance.

Jaime spoke in a low voice. 'It was Emilio.'

'Has he been in trouble with the policia again?'

'Not him. Emilio Loup.'

'Who's he?'

'Dolores is right, half your brain's become pickled. Ana's ex.

I met him in a bar when I dropped in for a quick refresher and after chatting I realized who he was.'

'What's he like?'

'Same as most. After a while, he got talking about her.'

'I suppose he cursed her for kicking him out of the feathered nest?'

'Said it was the happiest day of his life when he quit.'

'And the moon is made of blue cheese?'

'He said straight, he married her because of the estate, like you're going to do.'

'You think that's what counts with me?'

'Yes. The first night, she made it clear she wasn't interested in rumpy-tooting. That didn't worry him so much, not in the tourist season when one goes down to the beach and chooses. I can remember – before I married – I went down one night . . .'

'What are you talking about?' Dolores asked, as she stepped through the bead curtain.

'Discussing whether to watch a film that's coming on the telly,' Alvarez replied.

'Obviously, a film which should not be shown in a decent house. You may watch it, Enrique, if it gives you small pleasure, but my husband will not.' She returned into the kitchen.

Jaime spoke in a still lower voice and Alvarez had to lean forward to understand what he said. 'It wasn't her thinking he was constantly going off for a swim that caused the trouble.'

'What ended him was he got caught with a woman so Ana threw him out.'

'If you're going to tell me what happened, I'll shut up and leave you to shove your head into the sand.'

'If it wasn't woman trouble, what was the problem?'

'You know better than me.'

'Come on, lighten up.'

Jaime drank, replaced the glass on the table. 'It was how she went on and on. Did you put on a clean shirt; Elisée phoned and said that you walked straight past her in Carrer Sant Franscesc and you never apologized; I want you to drive me into Inca; tell the butcher in the supermarket that the beef I bought was tough; why do you want another hundred euros when I gave you a hundred at the end of last

week? . . . It became like he had to have her permission to
blow his nose. He took to drink and who'd blame him except
her? He had to buy it without her knowing because she
didn't like him having more than one drink before a meal
and a glassful of wine with it.'

'One?'

'And no coñac to aid digestion.'

'Yet when she was here, she said . . .'

'Which is what she told him before he married her and she
had him tight by the . . .'

'Have you rung her?' Dolores called out.

'I'm not certain it's a good idea,' Alvarez said.

'What stupidity is that?'

'She likes to go to bed early and I don't want to wake her up.'

'You cannot think of a more ridiculous explanation?'

'I'd rather leave it. If I ring this late . . .'

'It is not late and unless you are careful, she will think what
I think. That you are treating her as you did when she was
young.' She stepped through the bead curtain. She folded her
arms across her bosom. Her words were edged with icicles.
'I make one thing very clear. Do that and I will be so upset
at your cruel, monstrous behaviour, which reflects almost as
badly on the family as on you, that it will be best that you
find somewhere else to live.'

Alvarez watched her return to the kitchen. He faced disaster.
Either he accepted marriage which would prove to be far from
the rural nirvana he had been imagining or he would be
banished from home and Dolores' cooking.

EIGHTEEN

Alvarez sat in his car in front of Ca'n Mortex, his mind divorced from his body. He blamed Dolores for the impossible situation in which he found himself. She had introduced him to Ana; she had decided he should no longer be free and independent, here was the woman who would shackle him; she had cunningly induced him to see in Ana the reality of his dreams. Why did women never lose a chance to meddle with a man's affairs?

The sound of the front door's being opened brought his mind back. Roldan came across to the car. 'Are you all right, Inspector? You've been sitting there rather a long time. I wondered if you were not feeling well and you might like me to drive you to the medical centre.'

'No doctor can cure my problem.'

'I am sorry to hear that.'

Alvarez realized how selfish his mournful attitude must seem. 'Never mind me, how is Susanna?'

'No better, I am afraid.'

'So sad when someone is her age and cannot enjoy life.'

'Indeed. You wish to speak to the señor and señorita?'

'Unfortunately.'

Roldan allowed himself a brief smile. 'Perhaps you should hurry as I understand they intend to be out all day.' He opened the car door.

They walked into the hall.

'The green sitting-room is in the middle of being cleaned, so we'll go into the other one.'

'What colour is it?'

'I have never heard it given one.'

Smaller than the green room, it was furnished casually. Alvarez guessed the furniture spent time in there before moving on into the staff sitting-room.

'I will tell them you wish to speak to them.'

As Roldan left, Alvarez crossed to the right-hand window with a half-metre rock sill and stared out at the kitchen garden. Marcial was weeding a row of lettuces. A man who had known, as had almost anyone of his age or older, a bewildering change in lifestyle. He would have begun, a lad, working on a farm for a few pesetas a day, the hours long, burned by the sun or soaked by the rain, made to carry loads too heavy for his build; his only meal until the end of the day and he returned home, Pa amb oli; his home, a small, damp, dimly lit caseta which offered shelter, but little more since it had no electricity, no running water, no heating other than a wood fire, and only a long drop. Now, he worked for less time for many more euros, he ate his sandwiches and often a gourmet meal in the kitchen, would live in a new or restored house which had every amenity, perhaps including air-conditioning.

'How much longer do we have to suffer your insufferable intrusions?' Caroline demanded as she swept into the room. 'What the hell is it this time?'

'I should like to speak to your brother.'

'Why?'

'I will explain to him.'

'I demand to know.'

'After I have spoken to him, if he has no objection.'

'Are you trying to be even more insulting?'

'At least you allow, señorita, that unlike some, I have to try.'

'You are a mannerless peasant.'

'Peasants are expected to be mannerless, unlike English ladies.'

'You'll regret your damned insolence.'

'Hold it, sis.' Alec Sterne hurried through the opened doorway. 'If we're to reach Valldemossa on time, we have to leave now.'

'Are you going to let him talk to me like that without saying a word?'

'Come on.'

'I fear you cannot leave here until I have spoken to you, señor,' Alvarez said.

'We're meeting friends.'

'I will take as little of your time as possible.'

'Tell him to go to hell, we're leaving,' Caroline said angrily.

Alec's moment of determination was over. 'I can't do that.'

'Then I will.' She faced Alvarez. 'We are leaving now and you're damned well not going to stop us.'

'No, señorita, I will not. But you will be stopped on the road by members of Trafico and they will bring you back here. I shall then consider whether to arrest you both.'

'My God! It's the Gestapo.'

'I am forbidden to use thumbscrews. Please consider how much easier for all of us, señorita, if you will leave the room and allow me to question your brother quietly. After that, you may be free to leave as you will.'

Her voice was shrill. '"May"?'

'I have to learn what he has to say before I can be certain.'

'Are you so stupid you still think he murdered our father?'

'Had he done so, he would almost certainly have needed help.'

She was motionless for several seconds, her impotent fury making her face ugly, then she left.

'Shall we sit?' Alvarez suggested.

They sat.

'Señor, do you remember my asking you whether you had informed the Diamond Assurance Company of your father's death?'

A muttered: 'Yes.'

'What was your answer?'

'I . . .'

'You assured me you had not done so because you had been too emotionally upset. Are you able to judge why I asked?'

'No.'

'Had you murdered your father by making him fear for his life, it was very likely you would have taken the first opportunity to inform the company of his death so that you and your sister would benefit as soon as possible. That you had not been in touch with them was an indication, if far from firm, you were not implicated in his death.'

Alec Sterne was jiggling his feet; he fidgeted with the buckle of his belt; there were beads of sweat on his forehead.

'In a case this serious, I could not accept your word

without checking. I spoke to someone in the company and learned that you reported your father's death on the day he died. You have admitted you and your sister had reason to dislike him. You were in the house when he died. You lied to me over the question of informing the company of your father's death. You will understand I have to consider your position very carefully.'

'You . . . you're accusing me of killing him. I couldn't. I couldn't willingly hurt anyone.'

'Perhaps you were an accessory; even an unwilling one.'

'Never,' he shouted.

'Then explain why you lied.'

'I . . . I was scared . . .'

Caroline hurried into the room. 'What are you doing to him?'

'I am trying to understand why he lied to me, señorita.'

'He didn't. You hate us because of who we are. You'll try anything to blacken us and bring us down to your level.'

'Unless I learn there is someone else with emotional or financial reasons to wish your father dead, the effort may not be necessary.'

'You bastard!'

'That is never the fault of the bastard.' He left.

Back in his office, Alvarez noticed a sheet of paper on the desk. After a while, he picked it up. Sent by email was a list of the names and addresses of the owners of black hatchback Citröens with the registration letters, CIM, the owners of which lived in the northern end of the island. There were nowhere near as many as he had feared – only four. He felt slightly more cheerful as he phoned Franz Scabukle.

'Ya?'

'This is Inspector Alvarez of the Cuerpo General de Policia.'

Scabukle spoke a guttural, faulty Spanish. Fifteen minutes of troubled conversation established he had not known Señor Sterne, had not even heard the name before notice of the other's death had appeared in the local papers, had never visited Ca'n Mortex.

The difficulty of the call convinced Alvarez that the

remaining three owners should be left for another day – they might be three more linguistically challenged Germans.

'The superior chief will speak to you now.'

Alvarez waited.

'Yet again I have been expecting to hear from you,' Salas said without any greeting. 'Yet what is hope but deceiving?' There was a pause. 'Your silence continues?'

'I'm not certain what to say, señor. After all, hope isn't deceiving when it comes true.'

'The comment of someone unable to understand words which are not spelled out.'

'But how does one understand something which isn't?'

'Had I nothing to do for the next few hours, I would undertake the task of trying to explain. What do you have to tell me?'

'In truth, I suppose not very much.'

'One cannot accuse you of inconsistency.'

'The assurance company were able to tell me that Señor Alec Sterne was in contact with them within twenty-four hours of his father's death which is contrary to what he originally told me.'

'Have you challenged him with that fact?'

'I asked him to explain why he lied.'

'His explanation?'

'He didn't have much of a chance to offer one. His sister stormed into the room and made it impossible for me to continue the questioning.'

'You did not insist she leave? I find difficulty in understanding how an inspector in my command could behave with such pusillanimity.'

'Then it might be an idea, señor if you accompany me to Ca'n Mortex to question the señor further. Should the señorita again intrude, you could order her to leave.'

'I have no intention of doing an inspector's job.'

'It would be instructive.'

'I do not need to be instructed.'

'The señorita was most abusive.'

'To be expected, when you had clearly given her cause to be.'

'Señor, when she was rude to you, had you given her cause to be?'

'You seem to believe time is to be wasted, I do not. Have you managed to learn anything of consequence?'

'I phoned Herr Scabukle.'

'A personal friend?'

'He owns one of the cars on the list which has come from Trafico.'

'I recall no mention of such a list or of what are its contents.'

'It names black hatchback Citröens with the registration letters CIM. Herr Scabukle was the first name. It proved difficult to talk to him. He is a German.'

'As one would expect from the form of his address.'

'Ca Na Tortuga doesn't suggest a German owner.'

'In what feats of incomprehension are you now indulging?'

'Tortuga is Spanish for tortoise.'

'Am I to be expected to be grateful for the information?'

'I know it's not always a good guide to judge by an address when so many foreigners mistake the old custom of naming a new property with the nickname of the owner and use their own Christian names. But one can sometimes guess the nationality of the owner from the name. Of course, that only applies if the owner remains the person who built and named the property. In this case, I don't see that the name, Tortuga, gives any indication the owner is a German.'

'You have spoken at length, yet I have not the slightest idea why.'

'You said I should have expected to meet a German because of his address. I was trying to explain why that can lead to a wrong conclusion.'

'Your ability to misunderstand is only equalled by your inability to understand. His "address" was the form by which he is addressed. Herr denotes a German man.'

'It wasn't clear that was what you meant, señor.'

'No doubt it was the perfect clarity which confounded you. In order not to encourage further garrulity of no consequence, repeat the essence of what he told you.'

'He spoke German, which I don't, so we conversed in Spanish, kitchen Spanish in his case. Eventually, I was able to understand he had never met Señor Sterne or visited Ca'n Mortex.'

'And?'

'That was all I needed to know, señor.'

'You accepted his denials without question?'

'In the circumstances, it seems easier to question the other two first.'

'Convenience being of more importance than verification?'

'I would have to have a translator to question him efficiently.'

'No translator is likely to be able to help you do that.'

'If one of the other named owners did know Señor Sterne, had been to Ca'n Mortex, there would probably be no need to question Herr Scabukle again.'

'You have not yet questioned the other two owners?'

'I decided to report to you first.'

'On the principle I would appreciate learning you have carried out one third of your task inefficiently?'

'To tell you I was following up the evidence.'

'It is understandable that you cannot appreciate a member of the Cuerpo does not follow, he leads. Have you considered further lines of investigation?'

'I am going to pursue the married women.'

'You suffer no embarrassment when making so odious a statement?'

'I don't mean what it may sound as if I do. From the beginning of this case, there has been the probability that the husband of a woman Señor Sterne enjoyed . . .'

'As I have said before, you will not refer to an act of adultery as enjoyment.'

'Such husband had a very strong reason to threaten Señor Sterne violently, thus causing his death.'

'How many such husbands have you questioned?'

'So far, there has been no way of identifying any. I have repeatedly questioned the staff, but none of them has been able to provide a single name of a married woman who Señor Sterne . . . invited to his house.'

'Then how do you intend to identify them?'

'I don't know, señor.'

'You waste time discussing tortoises; you have not bothered

to follow one line of enquiry; you propose a fresh line while confessing you have no idea how to pursue it. Will you soon inform me you know who murdered Señor Sterne, but unfortunately are unable to name him?'

The conversation came to an abrupt end.

NINETEEN

Alvarez walked through the entrada into the sitting room. It was empty, as was the kitchen, but in there was the reassurance of a mouth-watering smell of stew. He remembered the children were away on a school outing, Dolores had said Jaime and she were going to visit an elderly friend who had recently returned from hospital after hip surgery.

He returned to the sitting room, brought a glass and a bottle of Soberano out of the sideboard, poured a generous drink. He fetched ice from the refrigerator, sat at the table.

He was discovering what drove a man to suicide. The choice between celibacy, teetotalism, and domestic slavery or moving into a rented flat which he would have to keep clean and tidy and his diet would be commercial meals from deep freezes.

The front door was opened and he heard Dolores ask Jaime if he had remembered to bring from the car, the magazine Rosa had given them. Jaime thought she had been going to do that. She questioned Jaime's ability to do anything before she entered the sitting room.

She glanced quickly at the bottle and glass. 'Lunch won't be long. But perhaps you will not be bothered when you eat.' She carried on through to the kitchen.

Jaime sat, opposite Alvarez. He filled a glass. 'Talk, talk, talk. The old woman went on and on saying how brilliant she was at crochet; the mayor of Palma had seen some of her work and said he thought it must have been done by angels. By someone half blind, more like.'

'Have you no sympathy for the old?' Dolores called out.

'Not when they repeat themselves for the fortieth time.'

'You'll be old one day.'

'A couple more hours of her and I'd willingly step into a coffin.'

'A woman understands compassion, a man never meets the word.'

'Didn't you say in the car she was an endless gramophone record?'

'Since she lives on her own, I was happy to give her the opportunity to talk.'

'And she took it with both tongues.'

'Enrique, Ana is coming to supper tomorrow.'

He emptied his glass.

'You have nothing to say?'

'What am I suppose to say?'

'You are so ignorant of warm words? You phone her immediately and tell her you've just heard she'll be along tomorrow and you can't wait.'

'Then she'll want to know why doesn't he drive to Son Cascall right away,' Jaime said.

'Even a childless wife has to look after a mewling infant.' There was a brief pause. 'You have no wish to speak to her, Enrique?' she demanded.

'Just going.' Alvarez went through to the entrada, across to the phone, lifted the receiver, waited, replaced it, returned and sat.

'You had so little to say?'

'The line's engaged.'

'You will try again in a minute.'

In his office, he opened the telephone directory, turned to the Porto Cristo section, searched through the Ns, hopefully found the one he wanted, dialled.

'Basil Nast speaking.'

'Inspector Alvarez, señor. Perhaps you will remember me?'

'If I may say so without causing offence, yours was a visit not easily forgotten. How can I enlighten you this time?'

'I should like to visit you tomorrow.'

'When exactly?'

'In the afternoon, at around six.'

'I'm afraid neither Janet nor I will be here. We're going on a cruise and fly to Italy at midday to pick up the ship.'

He would no longer have a valid excuse for not meeting Ana.

'Can you tell me now what the problem is?'

'Both you and your wife knew Señor Sterne well.'

'I, not as well as she.'

'Did either of you ever learn the names of other ladies with whom he was very friendly.'

'If we had done so, we would not repeat them to you. Not every couple enjoy the broad-minded attitude we do and we would not wish to be responsible for replacing a husband's ignorance with unwelcome knowledge. Am I correct to judge from your question, you do not yet know who killed Keith?'

'You are.'

'So you regard it most likely that an enraged husband was the guilty party?'

'That has to be a possibility.'

'And you chase all possibilities. No, Inspector, neither I nor Janet learned the identities of the many women with whom he had affairs. Surprisingly, considering his character, he made no effort to publicize his prowess in the sport.'

'No Christian names? No hints? You've never seen him in the company of someone else's wife?'

'He could be discreet where women were concerned.'

'I don't think that answers my question.'

'It's the only answer I'll give.'

'You do not wish to help identify his murderer?'

'If he was an unwilling cuckold, he has my sympathy, not hostility.'

'That is an unusual attitude.'

'Human relationships are never more unusual than when sex is concerned. Is there anything more you'd like to ask?'

'I don't think so, señor.'

'Then I'll sign off because I want a word with our travel agent to make certain our itinerary is correct. One of the local expats booked through them a trip by ferry and train to Brussels. He nearly found himself in Lyon. A meal cooked by Paul Bocuse would have lessened his annoyance.'

'I hope you have a happy cruise, señor.'

'It'll be a novel experience. Janet and I will be together all the time.'

The call over, Alvarez sat back. The odds against their being together all the time seemed remote. He considered his own problems. The staff at Ca'n Mortex had several times denied they could name any of the women Sterne had entertained. He would question them again, but had not reason to believe their answers would be any different. Sterne might have kept a record of his affairs; some men did. It seemed unlikely since Sterne had just been named discreet, yet he must prove to Salas he had done all that a man of enthusiasm and initiative would or could do. In the library, every book on the shelves should be checked in case it was a fake and contained the evidence he sought; all the drawers and files should be examined again because previously he had only really been looking for financial information . . .

'Did you phone Ana from work?' Dolores asked, as Alvarez entered the sitting room.

'I tried several times, but the line was always engaged.' He sat. On the television was a scene of some tropical island, palm trees, and flat calm seas. Live there and one would not be bedevilled by questions.

'I phoned her an hour ago and got through immediately.'

'Then it must be the phone in the office which is at fault.'

'More likely the person using it. Ana will be here tomorrow.'

'So you've said.'

'She is arriving at seven. You will make certain you are here to greet her.'

'If all goes well . . .'

'You will make certain it does.'

'I can't guarantee the superior chief won't suddenly order me to drive to Porto Cristo.'

She studied him, eyelids slightly narrowed across her dark brown eyes. 'You understood what I said? As much as I would regret your leaving here, however fond of you I am, you will no longer be welcome in this house.'

'You're trying to make something out of nothing. I never did anything to upset her when she was young.'

'Since you have said, very many times, that you cannot remember her, you cannot deny your behaviour.'

Seated at his desk on Thursday afternoon, Alvarez considered every possible move and discarded them all. Even if he persuaded a cabo to ring home to say he had been knocked over by a car and had been rushed to Inca in an ambulance, Dolores would need to view his battered body before she would accept he had been unable to return home to meet Ana.

Tens of hectares of rich land, almond trees by the dozen, orange and lemon groves, flocks of sheep; an unobtainable dream until now. Would it become a nightmare? Emilio had been denied the pleasure of her bed, of wine and coñac; he had been made to feel a servant, not the boss. Do this, do that; buy me a kilo of bananas; why weren't you back before eight last night; who was that you were talking to; do you intend to run this estate by sleeping every afternoon; I gave you a euro last week and now you want another because you sneak into a bar when I am not with you . . .

He could suffer his thoughts no longer. He must get out of the office to the freedom of the streets, order a brandy at Club Llueso and pay with money for which he did not have to account.

'You look like you've just been ordered to do some work.'

The cabo at the information desk was a graceless youngster. Alvarez walked along the narrow road, jostled by people of whom a large proportion were foreigners. They had chosen to leave their own countries for a holiday and no one had denied them the right to do so. The sunshine had the freedom to go where it wanted. The middle-aged man, dressed in a weird costume, enjoyed the freedom to make a visual fool of himself. The two young women in miniskirts proclaimed their freedom to display their long, slender legs, to grasp a man's gaze and yet scorn his advance.

He reached the old square, built up in the centre to provide a level surface. At the tables, under sun umbrellas, were people with the freedom to order what drinks they wanted.

'Inspector! Inspector!'

He stopped, turned, saw Marta supporting Susanna with an arm around her waist. He pushed his way through the crowd to reach them.

'Take us to the health centre. Quickly.'

He supported Susanna, shouted at people to get out of the

way, went down the short road, past the chemist to the taxi
stand – his own car was too far away.

Once the two women were seated in the rear of the first
waiting car, Alvarez draped a white handkerchief out over the
front seat passenger window – as a sign of emergency – and
jammed it in position by raising the glass. 'Drive like the devil
is chasing you.'

They entered the health centre through the outside emergency door. In the small waiting area, he rang the bell, knocked
repeatedly on the door. A nurse opened the door, began to
upbraid him for causing the disturbance, stopped when she
saw Susanna. She helped her into the examination room. Marta
followed.

Alvarez returned to the taxi. 'After that, I feel rather like
I'd been kicked in the nuts. Let's move to Club Llueso where
we can recover with a stiff drink, or two.'

'You being an inspector, I'm not drinking anything hard or
you'll have me in.'

'You have such small faith in me?'

'Having so much to do with you lot, I haven't any.'

TWENTY

Alvarez entered, walked through the entrada to the sitting room, came to a stop as Jaime, seated at the table, waved his hands in an unmistakable gesture to leave.

'Who is that?' Dolores demanded from the kitchen.

Jaime shrugged his shoulders.

Dolores came through the bead curtain, stared at Alvarez. Her expression was so bitter that his first thought was one of the children must have been injured. 'You believed I did not mean what I said?'

'About what?'

'You will leave this house. You will take out everything that is yours by this time tomorrow.'

'What's got you shouting?'

'You have the audacity to attempt to make out you do not know?'

'Yes, I have.'

'Ana arrived early because she had been told there was a shop in the village where she could buy what she wanted. She asked me where it was, so I said I would go with her. We were on our way when we saw you.'

'What's so frantic about that? Why didn't you come over and we could have had a coffee at one of the cafés.'

'You think sweet words can hide your cruel depravity? You think they can dry her tears, deaden her memory?'

'I don't know what you're going on about.'

'Liar! Accursed liar!' She put her hands on her hips, held her body forward as if a matador at The Moment of Truth. 'We sat at one of the tables in the old square and ordered two granissats. We had finished and were about to leave when we saw you with your arms about a young girl. And if that was not enough shame, she was pregnant.'

'That's nonsense. She's suffering from a virus which no one can cure.'

'You lack the courage to speak the truth? You have the infamy to refer to new life as a virus?'

'"New life." What are you talking about?'

'She is pregnant.'

'That's crazy. There are no signs of pregnancy.'

'You think a woman can't tell when another woman is pregnant when she looks at the face, the way she holds herself?'

'Obviously, you can't.'

'Did Ana weep bitter tears because she also was mistaken?'

'If . . . if you're right, you surely don't think it's my fault?'

'Why else would you embrace her?'

'Embrace? I was giving her support after her mother had called me to help. Now, I suppose you tell me I'm a cowardly, fornicating liar?' he said angrily. 'Then tell Jaime to drive you to Ca'n Mortex, speak to Susanna's mother, ask her how I can be the father when I had not met Susanna until the day Señor Sterne died.'

'You swear on your mother's honour, you are not the father?'

'You think me so licentious I would destroy a young girl's innocence?'

She slowly crossed to the table, sat. 'There has not been the time for it to show . . . But Ana was hysterical . . . Sweet Mary! but I am wicked to imagine such a thing possible. How can you ever forgive me?' She looked up in great distress. 'Drive like the wind to Son Cascall.' She spoke quickly. 'Explain how we were both shamefully mistaken. Assure her she has no reason to condemn you for anything . . .'

'No.'

'Do it, Enrique, or she will imagine you have betrayed her.'

'I cannot marry a woman who hastens to believe me guilty, who is so quick to condemn without cause.'

She spoke very slowly, as if having difficulty in finding the words. 'You are right. You would marry a woman who lacks trust, who cleverly conceals her true nature.' She stood. 'I must finish the cooking.' She went into the kitchen, her shoulders bowed.

Jaime brought a glass out of the sideboard, handed it to Alvarez, pushed the bottle across the table. 'You're a clever sod!'

'You think I arranged it?'

'How else could you keep Dolores happy and avoid Ana's trap?'

'Trap?'

'You never understood, but you're supposed to be the clever one in the family. It never occurred to you to wonder why she should have been eager to be so friendly with you when she told Dolores how despicably you had once treated her.'

'What stupidity are you talking?' Dolores asked, as she stepped through the bead curtain.

'I was telling him Ana was determined to get her own back, so she used the estate to lure Enrique into marrying her so she could reduce him to even less of a man than she did Emilio.'

'Only you could believe a woman would behave so cruelly.'

Alvarez awoke. The sunshine was coming through the shutters at an angle which indicated he had enjoyed a very long siesta, but he made no effort to get up. The pleasure which came from the solution of an insoluble problem was not to be lightly disturbed.

Not that it was undiluted pleasure. There was also pain, fear, death.

Unmarried girls who became pregnant were no longer regarded with hostile scorn, forced to wed at night. But Susanna's seducer must have disappeared or her parents would have forced him to marry her. An inspector in the Cuerpo was not expected to help an emotionally injured young woman, but when he recalled her, bewildered, depressed, defeated, he determined he would identify the boy and force him to act honourably.

He crossed to the front door of Ca'n Mortex. He knocked, when there was no response, knocked again. After a while, the door was opened by Caroline.

'What d'you want now?' she demanded.

'I wish to speak to Roldan.'

'The tradesmen's entrance is at the back.' She slammed the door shut.

Tradesman. On the island, that was an expression of worth. She had not intended it as such. He walked around the house. Roldan and Marcial were in conversation, of some emotion to judge by their hands and arms. They stared at him, then Roldan came down a narrow earth path between two rows of melons.

'Good afternoon, Inspector.'

'How is Susanna?'

'In hospital, but recovering.'

'I'm very glad.'

'Thank you.'

'Will you give her my wishes for a quick recovery?'

'With pleasure.'

'I'd like a word with you.'

'More problems, Inspector?'

'This is more a private matter.' He noted Roldan's sudden uneasiness. No father willingly talked about his unmarried daughter's pregnancy.

They went into the staff sitting-room. 'Can I offer you something?' Roldan asked.

'A coñac with ice only would be very welcome.'

He left, soon returned with two glasses, handed Alvarez one, sat.

'Your wife has told you about this morning?'

'We are very grateful for your help. Marta would not have known what to do without it. The virus sometimes affects Susanna very suddenly.'

'I have been told she is not suffering from a virus, she is pregnant. Is that true?'

'No!'

'I can have a word with someone at the hospital who will tell me whether or not that is so.'

Roldan drank.

'Is she there because of her pregnancy?'

Roldan finally nodded.

'There is trouble?'

'They . . . they think she may abort.'

A cruel solution, but a solution. 'Tell me who the lad is and I will get hold of him and make him accept his responsibilities.'

'You can't.'

'It may take time if he has scarpered, but . . .'

'For Christ's sake, why won't you understand? You can't.'

The despair and pain of a parent who feared his daughter had been seduced by a boy whose family believed they had the powers to protect him from the consequences? 'The name, Evaristo. If your worry is the boy's family, there are ways – moral pressure, the possibility of the truth becoming known and the adverse effect of this to the family.'

'Leave me alone.'

Alvarez hesitated, returned to his car. He picked up a pack of cigarettes from the dashboard, tapped one out, struck a match. The brief spurt of light ignited a different form of light in his brain.

Roldan had said, 'You can't,' as if in emotional pain. As Salas would pontificate, the meaning of 'can not' was to be unable.

He smoked as his thoughts reminded him how slow he had been. Only now did he accept the importance of recognizing that eyewitness evidence was notoriously inexact, often downright incorrect. So when independent witnesses gave closely matching evidence, it was well to consider the possibility their evidence was the result of collaboration. Roldan and Marcial had identified the car which had been at Ca'n Mortex as a Citroën hatchback; more significantly, each of them, and Marta, had referred to the dangling skeleton. Marcial claimed to have been badly shaken by the near accident with the outgoing car, so would he have noticed something so insignificant at a moment possibly of near panic? If he had, would he have identified it? Roldan had watched the car leave. At any distance, a dangling skeleton would become a something-or-other. Marta had noticed the car amongst heavy traffic and the dancing skeleton. Would she have done so when amidst a moving throng of people, trying to avoid collisions? She had noted the registration letters, but not the numbers . . . Did she have a sister whose initials were CIM? . . . Did that car exist only in the imagination of the three. Had it been invented to confuse? If so, could there be more than one reason why?

After Sterne's death, Roldan had been surprisingly, almost

subserviently polite, despite his own antagonism. Why? Had
Roldan and Marta had reason to hate Sterne?

He left the car, returned to the staff sitting-room. Roldan
was still there. 'The truth is, isn't it, that the father of Susanna's
baby cannot marry her because he is dead?'

Roldan said nothing.

'The body of Sterne is still in cold store so his DNA can
be determined and matched.'

Roldan spoke tonelessly, disjointedly. 'It meant nothing. We
thought he was showing some kindness. Because of all his
putas, it couldn't occur to us that the sod was interested in
someone of her age and innocence. We should have understood
that vice breeds on vice. The presents became bigger and more
costly. Now we were worried. She began to say how wonderful
it must be to be rich. Marta told her to trust a rabid dog rather
than him. We decided we must give in our notice and move
away. When we told Susanna, she said she would not go with
us. Then . . . We learned we had decided too late.'

Alvarez stood, put a hand briefly on Roldan's shoulder in
a gesture of commiseration, left.

He walked around the house to the kitchen garden where
Marcial was now cutting artichokes. 'I want to talk.'

'So what's changed?'

'We'll go into the shed and sit.'

'You may be bloody tired because you've been on your feet
for ten minutes, I've work to do.'

'We can talk in the shed where it's quiet and solitary, or
down at the post where it's noisy and everybody listens.'

Marcial picked up the cane basket in which were a dozen
artichokes, led the way to the garden shed, settled on one of
the two rush-bottomed chairs.

'Susanna is in hospital,' Alvarez said, 'facing a possible
miscarriage, not the repetition of a viral complaint.'

'You're talking shit.'

'It is to be hoped that a miscarriage is what she suffers.'

'Only a bastard inspector could say that.'

'Or one who believes it is the only solution to prevent lives
being ruined. You wish her to know her unwanted child was
sired by a libertine who seduced her with his wealth?'

There was silence.

'When did you first learn she was pregnant?'

'Didn't know she was.'

'You have always been fond of her. Marta has told me how you liked to talk to her, show her around the garden, explain how one needed to plant this here and that there. When you learned she was pregnant and that Sterne was the father-to-be, you hated the man as probably you've never hated anyone before.'

'The devil would have bowed to him. Wasn't content with all the married putas. The bastard had to have her as well. Why couldn't he leave her alone?'

'It seems there are no limits to evil, only to good. What did he say to you in the garage that Monday morning?'

'Didn't see him.'

'Were you bringing produce up to the house?'

'I said I didn't see him.'

'And I'm saying he was by his car in the garage and something he said or did triggered your fury.'

Marcial cleared his throat, spat. 'He said I was a fool to think he'd bother with a peasant's kid who'd likely caught pox from the last boy who'd enjoyed her.'

'Which made you so furious, you shouted you'd throttle his rotten life out of him and raised your hands as if about to do so. He fell, dead from fear. Scared, frightened, you went into the house and told Roldan. He said the police should be called, but they'd never believe you hadn't attacked Sterne. Evaristo is sharp. Knowing you had to prevent the truth becoming known, he said to lift the body in to the car and make it look like suicide.'

'You can't prove it,' Marcial shouted.

'I'm not going to try to. Even if you had intended to kill Sterne, I would have regretted having to charge you with his death. That you had no such intention, that he died from the shock of facing his own rotten self, there's no reason to charge you with anything.'

Caroline faced Alvarez. 'How dare you tell Roldan to order me to come and speak to you. I am here only to say that your

ignorant, crude impertinence will be reported to someone with
more authority than Superior Chief Salas seems to have.'

'Señorita, you and your brother will receive a large sum of
money from the assurance company. Some of that you will
give to a named person in order to avoid the publicity of your
father's being named as guilty of an immoral, criminal offence
before his death.'

'You're insane to suggest such a terrible thing.'

'An offence which any decent-minded person must find
abhorrent.'

'You expect me to give you money simply because of your
allegation?'

'If you can show more intelligence than you normally do.'
He was surprised when she did not shriek abuse at him.

'If you're trying to say he had affairs, he never denied that.
And there was nothing illegal about them.'

He had pondered how explicit he could be. If Caroline knew
who the victim was, she would dismiss her father's conduct
as impossible, would never accept her father had lowered
himself to seduce the daughter of his employees. 'The affair
was illegal because of the age of the victim.'

'Are . . . are you saying she was under the age of consent?'

'Yes.'

'You're lying.'

He was silent.

'You can't prove anything.'

'It can be proved beyond any doubt. You would not wish
to be known as the daughter of such a father.'

'You're trying to blackmail us.'

'The money will be paid to a notario who will be given the
name of the recipient, but who will not inform you of her
name; all you will learn from him is that neither I, nor anyone
connected with me, will receive a single euro.' With her regard
for status and distinction of class, she must agree. With the
loving help Susanna's family would give her, the money might
help her eventually to accept the past.

'Señor,' Alvarez said, receiver to his ear.

'Well?'

'I have a further report to make.'

'Then get on with it.'

As José Rubalcaba had written in his commentary on polit-
ics, the more bloated the lie, the more eagerly the throat widens
to swallow it. 'I have, with considerable difficulty, been able
to identify five of the married women with whom Señor Sterne
had affairs. In each case, it is certain the husband cannot be
considered a suspect. In my opinion, there is unfortunately no
chance of naming any other of the women. I have worked as
hard, and for as long, as anyone could, but nothing more of
significance has come to light, or is likely to.'

'You are admitting abject failure? The regrettably familiar
conclusion to any case you have conducted.'

The call concluded, Alvarez poured himself a glass of Soberano
to commemorate one of his more successful failures.